THE TRAGEDY OF KNOWLEDGE

RACHAEL WADE

CW01496457

ALSO BY RACHAEL WADE

PRAISE FOR AMARANTH

"A beautifully written story about love, sacrifice, and friendship that has a lot of fun twists and turns."
-Seeing Night Reviews

"As wonderful and enchanting as its beautiful cover..."
-Shadow Kisses Reviews

"...a new, exciting, and riveting tale of love and loss. The part that really stood out for me was that it is not just about fighting for your love, your soul mate, but it was about redemption of an entire clan so to speak."
-Alchemy of Annes Anomalies Reviews

"...I was hooked from the first chapter. I just wanted to step into the dark, dangerous world of Amaranth."
-Fiction Fascination Book Reviews

"A fantastic journey from beginning to end."
-Gothic Angel Book Reviews

"...far from 'just another vampire book.' "
-Live to Read Book Reviews

"Amaranth was in NO way a direction that my mind EVER would have gone. Talk about beautifully written, Rachael built a world that is absolutely stunning!"
-Taking it One Book at a Time Reviews

Rabbit Hole Press
Orlando, Florida
www.RachaelWade.com

Cover Design: Robin Ludwig Design Inc.
Editor: Arlene Robinson

Library of Congress Control Number: 2012949313
ISBN: 978-0-9840208-5-0 (Paperback)

DEDICATION

To anyone looking for closure. Acceptance is powerful.

ACKNOWLEDGMENTS

Many thanks to:

Dave and Patricia, the best support system a girl could ever ask for. I'm blessed beyond comprehension to have you in my life.

God, for His beautiful creation, forgiveness, and limitless love.

Book blogger and reader friends, for your enthusiasm, passion, and friendship. I love you all to the moon. Thank you for your support.

PROLOGUE

Amaranth, In the Beginning
Samira

Fury.

It was all I knew when he turned his back to stroll out of the room, and immediately, I knew it would consume me. I did not have a free will where it was concerned. Much as we are told we have a choice—a choice to love, to forgive, to accept—when you are the subject of choice, when it is your emotions you are to control and harness, free will slips away and the monster takes over. Desire and ability are conflicted. Whether I had an opportunity to surrender to its pull or rise above its ferocity, it didn't matter then, because fury's hand had already struck and ensnared me in its grasp.

"You will *pay!*" The words burst from my lips, and they instantly sounded weak. Desperate. Pathetic. Unsatisfactory. And yet they were all I could manage. He smiled and hesitated, then turned on his heel and disappeared behind the throne room's doors. My husband had not merely betrayed me with his selfish affair and trapped me here in this realm; he'd influenced and caused me to lose the one thing that meant more to me than any bond he and I shared.

Arianna.

As I stood there, staring down at Dali and Akim, I did not regret turning them to wolves. No. I'd reveled in the decision. It was the only one I truly had.

Everything was blurry, the throne room still and quiet, except for the sound of Erica's soft whimpers. Her sobs had transformed from heavy, wailing cries of grief to agonized, disbelieving whispers. I swished my wrist and snapped my fingers, and her husband vanished before her eyes, the pools of his blood disappearing with him, causing her to gasp and reach out as if she could actually stop him from disappearing. She sat slumped on her knees at the throne steps, rocking back and forth while she clutched her chest. It pleased me to dispose of Sean. He might have kept his promise to help restore my city to obedience, but it was not without a price.

Gérard had caught wind of my failure to control the people, and I could not bear to look at Sean's face—the face of my ex-lover's best friend—any longer. In addition, Arianna had fled the exile for earth during the uprising.

I'd never see her again.

I blinked and steadied myself, fighting the blurriness

that invaded my vision, waiting for it to pass. Each time I looked into Erica's eyes, some vague, uncomfortable ache bloomed in my chest, and I detested it almost more than I detested the sorrow I felt for taking her husband away. There was something else there, something that resonated with me so deeply, on such a human level, I feared I was losing my edge.

I was a frozen soul. A witch. A hybrid … a *queen*. None of those titles bent a knee to empathy.

Floating down the throne steps to stand beside her, I lifted my chin and gazed down at her, curious, working to place my feeling of discomfort. Her hazy, distraught gaze drifted up to mine, and the answer was there, in her bright irises.

Maternal love.

She was not merely mourning the loss of her husband, but the loss of her son. After I murdered her, Gavin would be orphaned. What would he learn of his parents' deaths? Would he have the luxury of closure? Would he know that his mother loved him? All of these questions were blaring loudly, right there in those pupils, and I couldn't stand the noise.

Bending down farther, I lifted her by the chin, feeling her frame tremble beneath me, and brought her to full height next to me.

"You think you know things," I whispered, "but you're really just asleep." Snapping my head to the side, I sank my fangs deep into the skin of her neck and let her drop to the ground, quickly reciting a chant over her body to prevent the venom from causing her to shrivel up and suck the life from her completely.

Her screams commenced, the burning from the transition evident. I motioned to the guards to seize her, and they lifted her off the stone floor and carried her to the prison tower, where I'd store her as my personal keepsake. Surely, she would remind me I wasn't alone in my betrayal.

Perhaps, as time passed, I could afford her the same comfort.

I

AVOIDANCE

"Damn it, Gavin!"

"Don't 'damn it' me, watch where the hell you're moving, babe!" The edge of his dagger pinned me in the shoulder as he encased me against his chest, the retractable blade slamming tight against my skin, closing against the handle. "You're losing focus. The second I come at you from this angle, you're already two steps behind me. You should've taken me down like yesterday." He pulled the blade from my shoulder and released my elbow, stepping back with a frustrated sigh.

"Hey, you need to cut a girl a break," I said. "I'm still new to this, and you're not exactly the best teacher."

"I'm not?" He stifled a smile, looking wounded.

"No, you're not."

"Well, damn." Narrowing his eyes, he placed his hands on his hips and scanned our surroundings, the wide-open field a lively green hue highlighted by the pink and orange sunset. We were attempting yet another combat training session, this one a few miles away from my little yellow Louisiana house I'd returned to after a three-month absence. For those three months, we lived in the realm of Amaranth, a place of exile for reformed vampires who'd been turned human again by Samira, the queen of the exiled. On the surface Amaranth sounded like a good thing for vampires—also known as frozen souls—who wanted their curses lifted. In reality, it was another curse. Once returned to human state, the frozen souls were kept there against their will to feed energy to Samira and her king, energy that kept them in power.

We'd returned to Amaranth with hopes of destroying Samira's kingdom and setting the frozen souls and Amaranthians free. We'd ended up with another mess to sort out. So, here I was, finally getting the chance to learn how to fight with the frozen souls' silver dagger weapons. The problem was, I seriously sucked.

Part of the problem was that Gavin was just too fast—and impatient—for me. The other problem was I couldn't stop ogling him while he taught me the correct techniques with the practice blades. Between his lean, tight biceps and muscular neck flexing against me during contact, his disheveled mess of hair, and the sweaty and torn white t-shirt that made him look like a bad boy from a rough neighborhood, my opponent and trainer was a drool-worthy mess of a distraction. Now that I was a frozen soul, even the lightest brush of his skin on mine ignited a tsunami of desire in me, a desire to feel him against, over, underneath, and inside me. Energy pulsed tight beneath my skin, vivacious and relentless, the need to be active and aggressive nearly suffocating.

It was all sorts of crazy. And a major disadvantage during training.

But I was getting used to my hypersensitive skin, the constant yearning to run long distances, and the desperate urge to launch into flight at every turn: a few of the new lifestyle traits that accompanied being a vampire. As for the twenty-four-seven crazed thirst for blood … that part, not so much. Gavin and his friend Gabe were still trying to help me get a handle on that one, and so far, were failing. Epically.

"All right. Look," he said. "I'm going to come at you again from the same angle—when you're not expecting it—and I want you to deflect my strike this time. All it takes is one stab of this silver, and you're instantly slowed down, do you understand? It can mean the difference between living and dying. One strike will make it easier for your attacker to land another strike, and then another. Each one making you weaker. Which means seconds until you're completely incapacitated. Then they can do whatever the hell they want to you. Think of it as paralyzing venom."

"Gavin. I got it. We've been over this." I pulled my hair tighter in a ponytail and wrapped it with an elastic tie, positioning myself in front of him again, knees bent, arms up, stance ready.

"Then get it together. I need you focused."

"Did I mention I really don't like your bossy side?"

"Did I mention I really hate that you don't do as

you're told?"

He met my stance with an amused grin, rubbing his hands over his shoulders to push up his sleeves. My gaze caught the movement, zoning in on his defined arms. I swallowed, and managed, "Do as I'm *told*?"

"Uh huh." He shuffled closer with slow, easy steps. "Out here, I'm not your husband. I'm not your lover. I'm your trainer. It's my responsibility to show you how to defend yourself. And it's your job to listen."

"I am listening. You just make it difficult … to stay focused."

"Oh, yeah?" He reached out and brushed a strand of hair from my forehead, letting his fingers trail slowly over my skin while he peered down at me, licking his lips. "Why do I make it difficult for you to stay focused, love? Are you having a hard time keeping up?" Pushing the hair back behind my ear, he leaned in farther, grazing his nose against my cheek, smirking when he heard me exhale a low, shaky breath.

Damn him. "You know why."

"Do I?" His grin widened.

"You do. And I won't give you the satisfaction of hearing it come out of my mouth."

"Cam," he dragged his lips across my cheekbone to the base of my ear, "I can feel it, too. You don't have to say it, because I'm in tune with your body like never before. We're on the same level now. All that pent-up energy, trying to claw its way out of you …" Nipping my earlobe, he let out a low chuckle and skimmed his hand underneath the hem of my shirt, tracing the waistband of my jeans with rough, teasing fingers. My entire body came alive at his touch, blood singing, knees quaking, mouth watering. His scent was divine and his lips called to me like some wicked, elemental magic.

He knew exactly what he was doing. The bastard.

More than willing to play along, I inhaled a sharp breath and reciprocated, dragging my fingers down his torso, then back up, stopping just above his navel. His mouth still near the base of my ear, his breath hitched against my skin at the contact. Encouraged, I headed south again, rubbing and teasing, feeling him grow beneath my fingers, tilting my head to the side to expose my neck. He moaned and grazed his teeth over my shoulder and down to my collarbone, dropping his blade to the ground with a loud thud.

"You make me crazy. Do you know that?" He gripped my hips and pressed me against him. "Do you feel what you do to me?"

"It's too intense," I whispered, my voice breathy. I was already panting when he moved to the other side of my neck, nudging my head to tilt it in the opposite direction.

"I warned you. You had a taste back in Amaranth, right after you changed." He started on the buttons of my shirt.

"But the pull is even harder to fight now. When you touch me … I have no self-restraint. Sometimes I feel like … like I can't handle all the extra energy. Like I'll detonate if I don't act."

"That's part of the fun."

"Gav … we're in an open field."

"Hasn't stopped you yet." He popped two more buttons. "I know you want me. Just relax and let me make you feel good, baby. That panic lessens when you give it an outlet."

Shutting my eyes tight, I leaned up on tiptoe and wrapped my arms around his neck to kiss him hard, then released him and slowly sashayed in the other direction, challenging him from underneath coy lashes, the need to run singing in my veins. "Fine. And I know *you* want *me*, but you'll have to catch me first."

His mouth fell open and his brows raised, a surprised smile pulling at the corner of his lips; he was ready to take the bait. I surged forward into a turbo-charged sprint, clear across the field toward the woods ahead, feeling him feet behind me, fast on my trail. I blew through the edge of the brush and into the thick marsh, lifting off my feet into flight, deeper and deeper into the bayou. This was what I loved: running full–speed, then transitioning into liftoff. The wind rushing over my sensitive skin, the way my body sailed over the ground below, with the speed of a bullet emerging from a rifle and a gazelle's grace.

The new ability exhilarated, even as it brought a pang of regret, remembering how I came to have it. After striking an alliance with our sworn enemy, Samira, our group caught the portal between her world, Amaranth, and ours, while it was still open, and left with the resistance to return to Louisiana to make new preparations. The resistance, comprised of rebel frozen souls on earth, and vampires-turned-human in Amaranth, formed a secretive movement to resist the vampire lifestyle that accompanied their curse; they didn't hunt or harm humans.

Our reluctant agreement with Samaria involved Gérard, Samira's absent husband, after we learned Gérard had a hold on her, using his magic to protect Amaranth and uphold his power. The only way to destroy that hold was to destroy its source. Simply bringing down Samira's reign wouldn't be enough to accomplish our goal.

Samira claimed she didn't believe it possible to destroy Gérard, and if she *was* privy to such information, she didn't seem interested in offering it up to us just yet. So Gavin and I decided to return to earth to visit Vivienne again, hoping her knowledge of hoodoo could help us, maybe even help find out if there was indeed a way to kill him. And to destroy Samira—our original plan—we'd need to find a way, because Gérard's magic didn't just control her, it protected her.

But when Gavin and I found Vivienne dead in her conjure shop, and discovered the warning Gérard left us there, the odds of us breaking the curse and becoming human again suddenly seemed worse, much worse. I hated what I'd become, and Gavin hated he was the one to turn me, but I was determined to focus on the positives … like enjoying my superhuman abilities.

With a soft crunching, my feet hit the dirt between

two majestic oaks nestled together on the side of the bayou bank. Before I had time to turn and scan my surroundings, Gavin landed behind me and forced me forward, flush with one tree's trunk, his front to my back.

"Oh, Mrs. Devereaux, you know how I feel about your teasing." His hot breath skimmed the back of my neck as he restrained me. Pulling my wrists together behind my back, he spun me around, bringing us face to face. He pinned my wrists above my head against the bark with one hand and unhooked my jeans button with the other.

"You gipped me out of a training session and went straight for seduction," I said between heavy breaths. "You deserved it."

He let out a low, husky laugh and yanked down my zipper. "Hate to break it to you love, but you making me work for it isn't punishment at all."

I squirmed against him, a moan escaping when he deftly dipped his fingers into my panties and inside of me. "Gav …"

His fingers plunged deeper.

"Gavin!"

"That's right, baby. Give it up for me. Come on." His palm tortured me as he flexed his fingers back and forth, squeezing my wrists tighter above my head with his free hand, keeping me restrained and helpless. I briefly resented that my strength still paled compared to his, even now, but when his fingers increased their rhythm deep inside me, I happily surrendered to his control. A garbled scream broke free from my lips as I rode out my orgasm, rocking my hips into him to capture as much of the friction as possible. His breathing was ragged now, his arousal digging between my thighs. As I rolled through the aftershocks, he freed himself and drove into me, fast, hard, and desperate. "You're a goddess. I adore you, baby. All of you. Always."

Matching him thrust for thrust, I gripped his upper arms and reveled in the feel of him, in the sensations that ripped through me as he dipped his head to bury his face in my breasts. My back arched against the tree, aligning my core with his, tighter and tighter, as we moved. I loved this man, this soul, my partner in life and eternity. It didn't matter what our future held now, or what would become of the frozen souls' fate because of our decision to join forces with Samira. Because whatever we faced, I'd have this man at my side, and I'd take a million silver daggers to the heart and an infinite amount of vampire transformations before I'd ever lose him or bring him harm.

Finding his release, he emptied into me, his jaw slack against my chest, his grip loosening around my wrists, letting them drop over my head and onto his shoulders. We leaned against the cool, damp bark, our bodies rising and falling against one another as our breathing calmed, the sounds of the bayou's eerie chorus surrounding us.

"How's that?" he breathed, his voice velvet on my neck. "Better?" Still panting, he propped his hands on the tree behind my head.

"Much ... better."

"*Mmmm* , agreed." With one last nip to my neck, he straightened and zipped up, offering me his hand. "Shall we, love?"

"What? I don't want to train now, can't we call it a day?"

"Nope. You were right. I gipped you. Back to work we go."

A whine of protest escaped my lips, but I complied, taking his hand. Before our bodies were air-bound, I glanced around, a thick, threatening aura engulfing my senses, the hairs on my neck spiking up. Suddenly it seemed the trees were watching, listening to our intrusion with acute focus, Gavin and me observers lurking in their midst. I shook the strange feeling off and let Gavin lift me into flight, sailing back toward the direction we came.

***

Gavin's house, a mansion that would have swallowed my little yellow house twenty times over, was quiet that evening. He only lived in a small portion of the house, the downstairs living area. I sprawled out on his sofa, trying to focus, to clear my head, itching to work on my novel, the one Gavin encouraged me to continue despite our outlandish circumstances. There was no going back to my house, no showing my face around town. Missing person's posters were plastered everywhere, courtesy of Carol, my former boss. The last time we'd checked on my place, the poor woman had even left flowers on my doorstep with a note. Seeing those made me feel even guiltier for leaving the way I did: with no warning, no sign that I was still alive. It must've scared her half to death to learn I really had gone missing after I disappeared from work the evening I supposedly went to take my break. But how could I explain to her, to any typical human really, that rather than returning to the bookstore that night, I in fact went to the bayou to enter the underworld of Amaranth?

But what was done, was done. I was back in Louisiana, at least, although I never really returned. It seemed as though one moment I'd been a human trying to conjure up spells while working at a normal bookstore, going to a normal college, and then was sucked into the paranormal realm and spat out as a vampire the next moment, before I had a chance to fully process the absurdity of it all. Then again, even at this moment, I could only process so much. If I let my mind linger on all the aspects of my transformation for too long, I'd start to lose it.

My fingers gliding across the pages of the journal, Gavin's gift, I recalled the terror that seized my body the day I'd seen it on the floor of Samira's throne room, the day we'd been summoned in Amaranth. *The day he changed me.* I shivered at the thought, thankful my friends and I had made it out alive.

Sort of.

Now everything was up in the air, with the resistance back in London, Paris, and scattered across the globe, waiting for a call from Gavin or Arianna, Gavin's sister, to find out their next actions. Waiting for some direction. Because now Gérard, the father of all the frozen souls—Samira's ex-lover and our worst nightmare—had sent us a gruesome message when we returned to Louisiana. One that made it clear he knew of our intentions to bring down Samira's reign, thereby destroying the Amaranth exiles, his main source of power. He'd ripped out poor Vivienne's throat and left us to find her in a puddle of blood, a revenge hex chanting on the ancient record player in the background. *Yeah, real subtle.*

Where he was lurking, we didn't know, but the fact that he was here, in Southern Louisiana, was enough to keep us all on edge. Putting it mildly. Since then, Audrey, my best friend, paced the house like a madwoman, cleaning and dusting everything in sight, while Gabe did laps around the outdoor grounds with his iPod on full blast, and Gavin in the kitchen, cooking gourmet feasts for them both. And me? When not training with Gavin, I attempted to write. Everyone was moving, but no one talked about the inevitable—what we would do when it was time to face Gérard.

Pulling myself off the sofa, journal in hand, I wandered over to the main hall, peering out the window to watch Gabe jog past the porch, screaming lyrics from "Bohemian Rhapsody" at the top of his lungs, most likely scaring off any birds and squirrels within a five-mile radius. Audrey flitted around me with the duster, appearing as a fairy sprinkling pixie dust, humming to herself as she did, and Gavin darted from the kitchen to shove a wooden spoon to my lips.

"Taste this sauce, babe. Too lumpy?"

I winced and jutted my head backward, licking my lips to taste the red goo. Human food wasn't quite my flavor anymore, but from what I could tell, it was fine. For a second, I wished I could crave his signature chicken parmesan again. But the craving for something warm and red quickly cancelled out the thought.

"Um, no. It's good." I shrugged. "Have Aud taste it. She's the human chef in the house."

Gavin glanced at her as she weaved around us, moving from one hall table to the next, dusting the wood a little too vigorously, fixated on one spot. "She's been a bit preoccupied lately." He cleared his throat, waiting for her to look over at us.

Nothing. Not even an absent-minded acknowledgment.

"That's it." I tossed the journal onto the table she was cleaning. The loud thud made her jump, finally stirring her from her obsessive cleaning frenzy. "We need a family meeting, Aud. We have to talk about this, because you all are driving me crazy. We're on a vampire conjure king's shit list, and he's in town. Right here, right now. Up close and personal. Stop your damn cleaning … and cooking," I eyed Gavin, "and music blasting!" Gabe couldn't hear me from outside, but it felt good to include his avoidance strategy in my outburst.

Audrey crossed her arms across her chest and cocked

a brow. "Well, someone's edgy. Gav, take her out to the bayou for your crazy monkey sex or something."

It was I who cocked a brow next. "Crazy monkey sex? We're vampires, not primitive apes. And how do you know we go to the bayou?"

"*Please* . You guys always sneak out to the same spot, giggling like hormonal idiots. Hey, I'm not complaining. When you do it in the house, Gabe and I have to hear everything. These wood floors and old walls are way too creaky for your escapades. I'm thankful you take it outside." She shrugged. "But you seriously need to do something about that attitude."

"I'm not the only one with an *attitude* around here." I lowered my gaze to her smartass stance. She shifted a bit, unfolding her arms.

"Okay, ladies. Tone it down a notch." Gavin stepped between us with a barely contained grin, the saucepan and spoon still in hand.

Audrey snatched the spoon from him. "Ugh. God, Gav, what, are you trying to kill us? Death by oregano? Give me that stuff. I've managed to rejoin the land of the living again, and I'd like to keep it that way, *thank you very much*." She yanked the pan away from him and charged past us toward the kitchen. Times like this, when she was her feistiest, I ashamedly entertained the idea of what life would be like had we left her in Amaranth. Gabe had turned her into a frozen soul early in their relationship, so she could enter exile with him and help carry out Gavin's plan to destroy Samira. Much to my amusement, it did nothing to water down her firecracker persona even now, after she'd returned to human form.

Gabe opened the front door with a loud huff as he pulled the iPod earbuds from his ears. Hearing the door slam, Audrey stopped when she reached the kitchen doorway and poked her head past the frame to point the wooden spoon at Gabe. "Get out of those clothes and into the shower."

"All right, now we're talking!" He gave her a goofy, eager grin.

Audrey handed the spoon to Gavin. "I mean it, Gabriel. You're all sweaty, and you're dripping all over my clean floors. Move it!"

His grin faded and he glanced down at his sneakers.

Gavin clapped him on the back and chuckled under his breath. "It's a madhouse in here, man. Come on, we'll grab you a beer. And I made you guys my chicken parmesan. Here, try this sauce." He shoved the spoon to Gabe's mouth—a little too forcefully—and with a mischievous laugh, turned on his heel for the kitchen. Gabe licked his lips and smacked Gavin on the back of the head with the spoon as he trailed behind, and I threw my hands up in the air, ready to strangle them all for their total disregard for our big, fat vampire-king problem.

We finally sat down to dinner, Gabe and Audrey chowing down, Gavin and me sipping our red, slushy nutrition.

"We aren't even sure it's Gérard who killed Vivienne,"

Audrey said, twirling spaghetti strands around her fork.

Gavin finished off his drink. "It's him. The record that was playing was an original conjure, and he's as original as they get. The date, and the initials on the record sleeve … it was all him."

"If it's anyone who knows him, it's Gavin," I said. "His dad and Gérard were BFFs back in the day, right, Gav?" I looked over at him, thrilled we were finally talking about this. Past time. I restrained myself from detailing why to the group, though it was difficult not to remind them it had already been three weeks since Vivienne was killed, and we couldn't hide out at Gavin's place forever. It was a miracle this conjure creep hadn't come for us yet. Besides, the next crescent moon was almost due, which meant it was time to act. And we'd be idiots if we acted without a plan.

"Well, it was my dad who knew Gérard," Gavin said. "I remember seeing him around the house every now and then, but I always stayed away because he creeped me out, even before my father began to mention the need to be cautious around him. Said he'd changed."

Gavin refilled his glass, and I could see his mind working, struggling with something. At last he said, "It's Arianna we need to talk to, but even she only knows him so well. Gérard brought her to live with my family when she was eighteen. But then she lived with Joel in London for a while, and then went back to Amaranth until the uprising. When she came back to earth again … human again from the uprising … her father couldn't be found.

No real surprise: Most frozen souls haven't seen him in centuries. So, she knows him as he was before she lost touch with him, but that's about it."

"So none of us really know what we're dealing with," Audrey said.

Gavin's expression turned grim. "I think the fact that he left Vivienne dead shows us what we're dealing with."

"So the question is, why hasn't he come to kill us all off yet?" Standing, Audrey started working her way around the table, clearing dishes and glasses as she went. "And why did he hunt Vivienne down in the first place?"

"To send us a message," Gavin replied, handing her his glass. "A warning. If he wanted to kill us, he would've. He went to Vivienne because he found out something was going on in Amaranth, that she was helping the resistance somehow. That's the only explanation. And Amaranth's portal is here. It's a hotspot for conjure activity. He knew to head straight to one of the original conjurers in town for answers." Brushing a hand over his jaw, he exhaled loudly. "This whole time, all these years, the resistance was sure that bringing Samira's kingdom down, draining Gérard's power source, would be enough to destroy them both, enough to lift the curse. He practically dropped off the face of the earth, and now he's here, and we can't destroy *her* without taking him out. *Unbelievable.*"

Standing, he sauntered over to the buffet table and grabbed a box stuffed full of loose papers. "Anyway, this is all we have from Vivienne's shop, all Camille and I could grab before we got out of there. We've been trying to piece things together since we got back, but most of the handwriting is illegible. She was on to something, but I still don't know what." He threaded his fingers through the box's contents, then set the box down and returned to his seat. "As soon as Arianna returns from London with Marie, we'll sit down and come up with a new plan. I've been training Camille with the knives, and I've told the resistance to use this time to prepare as best they can for whatever we face when we meet Gérard."

"And in the meantime?" Audrey's voice grew quieter, more uncertain.

"In the meantime …" He nodded to the box. "We keep trying to make sense of these remains, and hope like hell he doesn't show up before the portal opens."

Gabe shifted in his seat and reached for Audrey's hand. "I know it's not the most comforting thing to hear, babe. But Gav's right. If he wanted us dead, he would've come for us by now. Maybe he sees us as a legitimate threat."

"Either that, or we have something he wants," I said, the words escaping my lips before I had a chance to think about them.

"Maybe." Gavin eyed me curiously. "I'm not sure what we could have that would motivate him to keep us alive, though. Either way, it won't be long now. Arianna will be back from London tomorrow, and it'll be time to go back."

Time to go back. That thought silenced all four of us.

The quiet bore down around us in the dining room, the grandfather clock permeating it with a tired, taunting ticking. Discussing what to do about Gérard was only half the problem. There was still the issue of Scarlet, Gavin's ex, who had ratted us out to Samira while we were in Amaranth—and who was now on the loose, God knows where. Her jealous treachery had nearly gotten us killed before.

Added to that, our agreement with Samira was far from comforting. She still had Gavin's mother held hostage back in Amaranth, and for all we knew, she could flip a switch on the agreement and turn her back on us, or worse, send a message to Gérard to take us out. Or worse still, take Gavin's mother's life for real this time.

These possibilities hung in the air like thick smoke, and the need to run flooded me with urgency. Rising to my feet, I darted out of the dining room and out of the house, sprinting across the oak tree-lined driveway and into the night, hoping Gavin wouldn't follow. I needed the quiet, needed to think. And there were those pesky daydreams to mull over, the ones that caused me to black out like I was sleepwalking. They began right after I'd changed and were getting more frequent, more inexplicably terrifying. All I could see as I replayed the scenes in my mind was Gavin's mother's room. The indentation of my crescent moon necklace on the bed's pillow. The skeleton key that unlocked her door. That dream meant something, it must!

Instinctively, I clutched the necklace tight in my hand as I ran deep into the bayou and let it enfold me in its darkness.

2

FIRESTARTER

"So … how was it?" It sounded like the stupid question it was, but I didn't know what else to say.

"It was okay." Arianna shrugged petulantly, sliding a box of Joel's belongings onto the kitchen counter. She'd gone with Marie, Joel's mother, to his old apartment in London, hoping to salvage some of her memories with him so she could move on. Marie stood next to her, hands folded in front, a wary expression that defined the wrinkles on her face. Marie left Amaranth with us and the rest of the resistance, still marked and owned by Samira, but given permission to exit Amaranth with us to help prepare for our attack on Gérard. Samira wasn't happy about Marie leaving, but Arianna insisted, and so she complied.

"Did you get everything you wanted?" I said.

Another shrug. "I guess. I found an old photo album of us. And some records I gave him on his birthday." She pulled the album from the box and stared at the cover, a single tear spilling onto her cheek. My heart constricted at the sight, and then my eyes widened in surprise when Marie reached over a hesitant hand to stiffly rub Arianna's back. Arianna's sobs deepened at the contact, her face falling into her hands. Marie moved closer to shush her, tears of her own spilling over her eyelids.

I reached out and gently squeezed both their shoulders, my voice quiet. "I don't know how. But we're going to make this right. We'll end this."

"How can we ever make this right?" Arianna's voice cracked through her sobs. "His death will never be right. There will never be any justice. The odds against us are stacked so high, I don't see how …"

"There, there, child," Marie whispered, sending me a worried glance. "Your spirit is broken right now. But not lost. There's no room for giving up hope, do you hear me? He was my son. Can you imagine the depths of my sorrow over his loss? The pain it brings me to know I've been a slave to your mother, the one who is responsible for the loss?"

Arianna turned to face her, her long golden curls brushing against Marie's shoulder. "And do you know what that knowledge does to me? It's devastated me, Marie. My mother, a monster, took him from you. From me. She made you pay for his freedom, for his visitations … not to mention that this all began with my father. I can't possibly put into words how sorry I am. I feel responsible, I feel—"

"No." Marie took Audrey's chin between her fingers. "You are not responsible for what your mother's done, or your father for that matter. You never were and never will be. You gave my son happiness, a life! He adored you. I was wrong that day … the day at the gates, when he came to see you. I never should have gotten involved. It was all just too much for me to bear. To watch you two fight, to see what my son had lost when you returned to Amaranth. I couldn't see how your relationship would ever work with so much against you like that, and I didn't want my son to continue torturing himself over his decision to stay on earth, to remain a frozen soul."

Arianna and Marie stared at one another, a bittersweet silence passing between them: Arianna's head bowed, hand cradling her chin; Marie's knowing eyes brimmed with tears, her grip on Arianna's shoulder gentle. It was heartbreaking to see, yet a relief to see them come to an understanding. Marie might have been a monster, one that tried to capture me and return me to Samira not long ago, but seeing her maternal side, her love for her son and her desire to make peace with Arianna, made me reconsider my early opinion about her heart. Her position as Samira's slave all these years, and what it must have meant for her. I instantly added her to my mental list of those I wanted to protect, to fight for in this war against Gérard and Samira. To the death.

"I'll give you guys a minute," I said, my voice still quiet. They turned to me, expressions solemn, eyes tired. "I'm going to go see what the guys are up to." With a wry grin, I exited the kitchen in search of Gavin and Gabe. Audrey was out running errands, so it was just the boys and me while Marie and Arianna had their moment.

I found Gavin in the living room, pinning pieces of the remnants from Vivienne's shop onto a pegboard. He'd assembled four full-size boards on the wall near the piano, rafted them together to create one mega-sized board for putting the puzzle pieces together. Papers littered them, overlapping with one another and spilling over onto the surrounding wall.

"Hey, love," he glanced over his shoulder. "How is she?"

"A mess. She and Marie need a moment, so I stepped out." I crossed the room and came to stand next to him. "So … you and Arianna talked earlier. What's our next move?"

He pinned another shred of paper to the board in front of us, dragging his index finger along the edges as he studied it. "Well, when we get back to Amaranth, we'll break the news about Vivienne to Samira. Hopefully, hearing who we think killed Vivienne will bolster Samira's resolve to go after Gérard. Maybe she'll have a plan of action in mind that we haven't considered. We'll join forces with the rest of the resistance, and the Amaranthians, to face him. When we left Amaranth to come talk to Vivienne, I was hoping she'd have some clues as to how we can kill him, or how we could garner more help from the conjure side of things. I've come to the conclusion that if she did know anything, she would've told us the last time we saw her. Whatever she was on to here, we were all too late."

"Do you think there are any other local witches ... any originals ... who could help us?"

"I don't know. Possibly. Unfortunately, I have no way of getting in touch with any of them, even if they are out there. From what I understand, Vivienne was the only one who operated in town, who engaged with the locals and even bothered to help our kind. Most of the witches reside deep in the bayous and keep themselves sheltered, knowing the area is rich with frozen souls. We're a threat to them, we're the enemy. Their magic can't harm us, only that of our creators can. That leaves them at a disadvantage. And as Vivienne explained to you, they don't think very highly of Gérard and Samira. We're guilty by association. The only other thing we have is the witches' Book of the Ancients. I've been studying it, but it doesn't reveal an ending to this mess. It only points to the water and snake prophecies, and some of the history between our kind and theirs. The last few pages are completely blank, as if ..."

"The ending's yet to be written." Turning to sit on the piano bench, I let out an exhausted sigh, recalling the blank pages back when I'd first acquainted myself with the book in Amaranth. "So we're at a dead end."

"Not entirely, babe. What I can't understand is what Vivienne found that made her panic. Looking at the papers that were on her counter, it seems she was scribbling and writing so fast, her mind couldn't keep up. Some of the ink was fresh. And look at some of the writing, how it abruptly stops, the sentences unfinished.

Whatever she was trying to do, we were just too damn late to help her."

"I wish I could tell you. Here, let me help. Two minds are better, and all that." I pushed myself off the bench and resumed my place by his side, shuffling through the box of papers. We moved things around on the pegboard, squinting to read some of the pieces aloud, exchanging ideas as we went.

"Hey, I've been thinking." Gabe's voice came from behind us. He sauntered in wearing the same workout clothes as yesterday, again soaked in sweat, iPod earbuds hanging from his ears. Gavin and I turned to meet him. "I'm out there for my run every day, right? Blasting my music, trying to make sense of all this crazy shit and how we aren't getting anywhere. We're like sitting ducks, just waiting for him to come and get us, or go after others in the resistance. And we don't know what we face if he shows up at the portal. I mean, this conjure dude obviously wanted to scare us. Goal accomplished. But, so what? We're already scared. All we have are dead friends, promises we can't trust, and these," he shuffled forward and shook the box of papers, "nothing but jumbled-up clues to show for it all. I say it's our turn to scare *him*. So screw sifting through all of this stuff, wasting all this time. Let's invite him over and turn the tables. Be done with it, so we at least know what we're dealing with before we show up at the bayou."

Oh, how I admired Gabe's straightforward tenacity. But it would get us killed.

Gavin relaxed a bit, tucking his hands in his pockets with a tight smile. "I wish we could, man. But the reality is we can't afford to just have him show up while we're unarmed, unprotected. We have to figure out his weakness if we want to have the upper hand when it's time for the showdown. Otherwise we're just digging our own graves."

"What about the spell Vivienne helped us cast?" I asked, crossing my arms over my chest. "The one that gave us protection and energy when we went to Amaranth?" While the frozen souls couldn't be affected by human witches and their magic, the ability to use their magic amongst their own kind was a nice advantage of being bred by two hybrid creators. But it didn't help when we had no idea how to use it, and no witches willing to show us how. Only Vivienne offered her help, and that option was out.

"We still have Vivienne's instructions for it, but it's not like other spells. It's too big for frozen souls to cast on their own. We'd need help—a direct connection—from an original witch again." Gavin nodded to the box. "And I don't know any other original who will agree to do what Vivienne did for us. It's too risky for them to help us. Now I'm just trying to find another angle to work from, one that will give us an advantage over Gérard somehow."

"Well, I still say let's give him an invitation," Gabe huffed. "What else can we use as ammunition?"

The three of us exchanged glances when the sound

of footsteps interrupted our thoughts. Arianna appeared in the doorway, wiping her nose with a tissue. "Did you guys figure anything out?"

Gabe cut a glance to Gavin, a question in his eyes. My stomach dropped, not liking the look on Gabe's face. Arianna must have noticed, because her gaze bounced from my face to his, her eyes narrowing in suspicion.

Gavin growled low in his throat but held Gabe's gaze. "The answer's no. She's been through enough. Don't even think about it."

"Arianna, yeah, we might've just figured something out." Gabe's voice carried across the room, as if making it extra clear Gabe was ignoring Gavin's warning.

"Damn it." Gavin pierced Gabe with a cutting glare, then turned his attention to his sister. "Ari, I hate to ask, but—"

"We need you as bait. And a bargaining tool," Gabe spat. Gavin's eyes snapped shut at his words. "How would you like to see dear old Dad again?"

"More like we need you for protection," Gavin clarified through gritted teeth.

"Yeah, insurance. Whatever." Gabe shrugged. I stepped back a bit, wincing at the delicate way the boys had delivered the blow. As much as I hated to admit it, the idea was a good one. Arianna was likely the only one in this room Gérard would think twice about before harming. Using her to our advantage might be our only hope, since it seemed we had nothing else.

"Wait," she said, chuckling and her eyes rolling to the

ceiling. "Let me get this straight … you want to use *me* as a weapon when we confront my father? I'm all we've got?"

"Afraid so," Gabe mumbled, hanging his head, finally showing a little shame for his suggestion.

Gavin took a step closer to her. "I know it's been a long time since you've seen him, Ari. And I know how you feel about him. But we're not getting anywhere with Vivienne's old stuff. We don't have any magic to help us, and there are no clues in the witches' history to help us figure out how to bring him down."

Arianna let out a long exhale. The four of us stood there for a moment, until she finally broke the silence. "Fine, though I doubt it'll do any good. What's your plan if we don't even know how to kill him? If he already knows we're after him, he might've also caught word that I'm on your side." I breathed a sigh of relief at her permission, relief I saw that Gabe and Gavin shared. But then the worry settled in. The quiet filled the room again, and Gabe wandered over to the wall to study the pegboard while Gavin stumbled off, his face clouded with thought. I stood there twiddling my thumbs, eyeing the exit, itching to go for a run.

"We'll have to confront him and make a deal somehow," Gavin finally replied. "Use you as a bargaining chip, the same way we used you against your mother. If he does know you're on our side to destroy him, maybe that'll be enough to thwart him or something."

"Ha." Arianna laughed again. "Thwart him into what?

Into him giving up all his power in exchange for my forgiveness? For a relationship with me? For my safety? Yeah, that won't happen."

"Maybe not, but it's worth the risk. Play the same card with him that you're playing with your mother. If he has even an ounce of parental guilt, he'll at least consider it. Your mother did."

"Gav." She strode across the room to meet him at eye level. "My mother, as evil as she is, is ridden with guilt. That emotion doesn't even register on my father's radar. 'Hey, Dad? Can you please stop holding innocent people captive in your fairyland hellhole to feed your power, and while you're at it, lift the vampire curse? *Mmkay?* Thanks.' Don't you think if I could've said it a long time ago, I would have? If I thought for one second my request would've meant anything to my father, that would have been my first priority. I'm telling you right now that he couldn't care less about making things right with me. Especially not when it involves his power. It fuels his ability to be in charge. And that's what he wants, why he and Samira created the frozen souls in the first place. I'll be of no use, trust me. Besides, he wanted me to choose to become a frozen soul on my own, remember? And I did, to be with Joel. He'll be less than thrilled to learn that I changed my mind. Not just that, but that I want to lift the frozen soul curse for everyone and destroy his precious creation. If you think you can use me somehow, more power to you. But that won't work."

Gavin opened his mouth to respond, but Gabe's voice

stopped him. "That might be the case. But we might have something else to work with." He delicately grabbed three pieces of paper from the board on the wall. "Here. Look at this, guys. Did you catch these names?"

The four of us huddled together around the piano, Gabe assembling the edges of each piece to push the words together. "There's something here about Dali and Akim. Aren't those—?"

"My mother's wolves." Arianna leaned in closer to study the rest of the papers. "My dad's old conjure mates. What about them?"

"I don't know," Gabe said. "Vivienne's handwriting runs out, like the rest of the sentences she was trying to write...."

We tried studying the text a while longer, but it was no use. Letting out a frustrated sigh, Arianna turned for the door. "Gav and Cam, keep digging and see what else you can find. Gabe, you and I are going to put a plan together to lure my father here, and Audrey can help us when she gets home. We're going to round up the troops for backup and bring them here first, though. Come on."

Gavin said, "Ari, wait—" but she was already out the door, Gabe trailing after her with a resigned shrug. Gavin and I resumed our research in silence, the grandfather clock's ticking echoing from the hall, grating on my nerves with each dismal stroke of the hand.

***

"Cam? Hey, Cam, hello?" Audrey's voice echoed

through my post-daydream haze, once again breaking me from my trance. I found myself in Gavin's mother's room, sitting at the small writing desk against the window, elbow propped up and chin in hand, as if I were gazing out to admire the view. "Cam, can you hear me? Arianna has word on the resistance, we're waiting for you downstairs, come on."

"Aud?" I kept my back to her, gaze out the window, still adjusting to the return from my hypnotic state.

She let out a soft sigh. "More visions?"

"Why is it only me this is happening to? I mean, you didn't see things when you changed, right?" I shifted in my seat, meeting her eyes over my shoulder.

"I don't know why. I wasn't a frozen soul for very long. Aside from the blood cravings and the intense need to run around like an Olympic gold medalist, I didn't experience the full transition like you are. No mind-speak, never got in touch with my energy-reading abilities, never found out what kind of mortal emotion I can read. … I wish I had an answer for you."

"Cecile never mentioned anything when you spent time talking with her about her history as a frozen soul?" Cecile, Audrey's long-lost aunt and a human-turned witch, was another casualty during our time in Amaranth, and it still hurt to think about that.

"Nope, nothing about visions or dreams that I recall. Are you still seeing the same things?"

I glanced back out the window again, shaking my head. It was all still the same: the skeleton key, his mother's room, the search for the necklace on the pillow, though it remained safely around my neck. Just as I began to give up on the frustrating puzzle, my entire body stiffened, the hairs over my arms and neck on red alert. A piercing scream echoed from downstairs and I shot to my feet, launching myself toward Audrey, stumbling and losing my balance. Her eyes met mine, widening when she reached out to catch my elbow. Struggling to regain my balance, I leaned against her, chest heaving from the overwhelming ball of heat emanating from my chest. It thumped hard against my ribcage, vibrating and threatening to steal my breath.

"Camille! Oh my God, Cam!" Audrey's voice lost its clarity, splintering into a thousand glass shards and bouncing off the wooden floors, puncturing my hearing with a shrill pitch. My hands protectively clasped my ears and again I fell to my knees, the ball of heat pounding harder into my chest. "Can you stand up? Are you okay?"

Audrey frantically glanced between me and the bedroom door while dragging me out into the hall and toward the staircase. My vision blurred as she guided me, then cleared as it locked onto a dark brown man, who stood near the front door at the bottom of the staircase.

How I'd ever imagined Samira to be the definition of evil incarnate was beyond me. Because the man who stood before us held that title with fierce superiority. Where Samira carried a vast amount of sexuality in her demeanor and body language, this man dripped with an insurmountable, carnal, wicked sensuality: a manifestation of deceitfulness, the serpent of the Garden of Eden; a suave creature dressed impeccably in a French gray suit, no tie, relaxed cuffs and crisp, matching fedora, ready to strike its prey. He removed the hat when he met my gaze with dark eyes that matched Arianna's, an inviting grin playing across his lips. I drank in his sophisticated appearance, and one look into those dark, savage eyes told me all I needed to know: Sex was his weapon. He didn't need to rely on grisly, monstrous features to instill horror; it was all there, in his self-assured stance, and in those wild, smoldering eyes.

I immediately sensed Gavin, Gabe and Arianna gathering in front of him at the end of the staircase, their stances at once stilled. And defensive. As he held my stare, the thumping bomb of heat radiated with more ferocity, causing me to grip my chest with terrified, rigid fingers. Was I the only one feeling this? The man's eyes, the sinister undertone in them palpable, glittered with amusement as I fought to steady my breath.

Silence fell around us, and suddenly, I realized the source of the horrific scream we'd heard. Marie lay lifeless at the man's feet, a trickle of maroon dribbling from the corner of her mouth, her arms and legs shriveled. Every muscle in my torso contracted at the sight that reminded me of the ghastly way Andrew's body looked the moment Samira had bitten his neck, sucking the life out of him and leaving him a desiccated, rotting corpse.

The man tore his gaze from mine, casually turning his attention to Gavin. Smooth words tinged with a mischievous yet chilling, seductive Creole blend, spilled from his lips. With a snap of his fingers, a lit cigar appeared between his index finger and thumb. An exotic aroma of burning incense drifted up the staircase toward me as he took a puff. Audrey and I froze at the top of the stairway, unable to move while he spoke.

"*Mmmmm,* I'm very unhappy to be here, Gavin," he said. "Do you know why that is? Because I don't like to fly, you see. I loathe it, in fact. I don't like to travel. I've seen every inch of this sorry excuse for a planet and frankly, it's boring. I'm very comfortable in my Moroccan palace. So, my friend, to come here, it's a quite significant inconvenience for me. Quite."

Taking another slow, tantalizing draw from his cigar, he tossed his hat onto the hall hat tree's hook, strolling forward to peer around. His dark fingers flitted around as he spoke, fingers embellished with numerous gold rings, the bright yellow flashing under the room's natural sunlight. A woven straw bracelet of some sort dangled from his wrist and he toyed with the attached charm a moment before dipping his hands in his pant pockets.

"Father." Arianna's voice was surprisingly squeaky, a sign that there was in fact fear beneath her tough exterior. "Get on with it, already."

"Ah yes, my beautiful girl. Straight and to the point as always. I do admire your direct approach." His eyes flickering to mine once more, they lowered, settling on my necklace, and then lower, on my cleavage.

I swallowed hard.

"Gavin, my friend. I'm so sorry to hear about what happened to your parents after the uprising. When I learned that Arianna left Amaranth during all the commotion to return to earth, I also caught word that Samira requested your father's help to put things back together, and well, I knew that meant I'd need to come and clean things up. I also knew your mother would leave earth to join him there, to help him. The way Samira lured your father into serving her, by lifting your mother's curse and granting her admission as a human," he shook his head with a disapproving look, "well, that was just cruel. Alas, my ex-wife never could exercise control, the fool. What nerve, to later try and cover up their murders to keep it hush-hush."

Oh, how nice of Samira, I thought. *Giving Gavin's mother her humanity back, only to change her again after she used and discarded her husband.*

Her monstrous nature really did know no bounds.

Visions of the tormented expression that graced Samira's face when she'd seen Arianna after all those years, right before we'd left Amaranth, popped unbidden into my mind, but I swiftly extinguished the irrational wave of sympathy.

"It's a pity Samira's weakness caused a rebellion in her city," Gérard continued, and looked directly at Gavin, "and my, how proud Sean and Erica would have been to see what a strong, determined young man you turned out to be. They were dear, dear friends."

Finally, Gavin's mother had a name: Erica. And

apparently, Gérard didn't realize Samira had kept Erica around after all.

The muscles in Gavin's neck tightened and released, his jaw setting at Gérard's words, but his lips remained clamped shut. To think that Gavin's father was ever friends with this man sent more tingling sensations down my spine.

"Funny, Father." Arianna's voice was stronger now. "It seems Mother's been exercising control just fine. Plenty of innocent people are still being held captive in *your* rebellious exile. I'd say she possesses another strength, in addition to her ability to play gatekeeper. She's an excellent janitor, cleaning up *your* mess."

The heels of Gérard's dress shoes lightly clacked on the wooden floor as he shifted. From just outside the open door, the front porch's wind chime faintly tinkled. No one moved. "Ah, defending your mother, are you?" he said. "Last I heard, you weren't so fond of her, my beautiful girl."

"Last you heard? Some time has passed since then, *Daddy.*"

Gérard sucked in a sharp, over-dramatic breath and screwed his eyes shut, as if someone had delivered a punch to his gut. "That's hitting below the belt, baby girl. But I do understand your animosity. It's true I haven't been around, and it seems some things have changed, yes?"

A tear streamed down Arianna's cheek as she eyed Marie's lifeless body. Gavin's gaze shot over his shoulder toward Audrey and me. Arianna's dress bristled as she shifted, the grandfather clock's ticking echoing from the corridor.

"But you are right. I should get to the point." Removing his free hand from his pocket, he retrieved a long silk handkerchief and rubbed it over his fingers to wipe away Marie's blood in between healthy puffs of his cigar. "Do you and your friends here know why your mother and I are the only true hybrids? Why we have the strongest powers, possess the best of both worlds from the frozen souls and the witches? While the frozen souls rejoice in the knowledge that they can perform silly little magic tricks and cast pathetic spells amongst their kind, your mother and I have conjuring abilities they merely dream of." Stepping over Marie's body, he angled his chin lower, keeping his eyes on his daughter. "Well, do you know why that is?"

More tears ran down Arianna's cheeks; her silence brought another flippant smile to his face.

"It is because I am the *author* of the frozen souls. You see, years ago, the witches' magic had so much potential, so much promise. It was grossly underused. Ah, but when paired with the abilities my curse had to offer, well," he chuckled, "that is God incarnate, baby girl. Immortality and the power to manipulate, to protect, to acquire all that you wish, whenever you wish. Hard to call it anything but a blessing, then, wouldn't you say? You cannot blame Daddy for wanting to be in such a position, now can you?"

Audrey's fingers trembled beneath mine as we both fought to hold one another up, our shaky knees knocking next to each other and hands locked. If there was any time I truly wished to read Gavin's thoughts and speak to him through mine, now would be that time. I silently sent my thoughts to him, willing him to hear me. No reaction. I'd been told I was still too young a frozen soul to develop the ability, that the bond with my small coven was still too new to break through just yet. But it didn't deter me from trying.

"As the author of something, I have a say over what happens to my characters, my creations," Gérard said. "I set the stage, feed them their lines, determine their purpose. So, you see, no magic the frozen souls try to use against me or my kingdom will compare to what your mother and I can do. Because I alone determine to what degree that magic can be used. Quite simple, yes? And now, as the *author* of all you … characters … who wish to destroy my kingdom, I choose to end your purpose, since you seem to be interested in perverting it."

With a small, subtle swish of his wrist, Gérard pushed Gabe, Gavin and Arianna backward, until their backs slid against and pinned to the hallway walls, carving a path straight up the stairway to Audrey and me. He snapped his fingers and the cigar disappeared, his arms dropping smoothly to his sides. The heat over my heart flared, coiling up into a beating drum while Gérard waltzed up the stairs toward us, eyes holding mine, then spread south, just below my hips, leaving me weak-kneed. Audrey tightened her grip on my arm to help keep me vertical. My fingers dug harder into my chest as I gripped the pulsing spot, the edges of Gavin's mother's necklace grazing the tips of my fingers.

"So, my friends. I declare a new act. You tell everyone in this *movement* of yours to report to the bayou portal when it opens tomorrow night, and I will kindly escort you all to exile where you'll spend the remainder of your eternity—your human friends included—" he glanced over his shoulder to peer down at Gabe, "or I personally hunt you all down and rip out your hearts, one by one, until there's nothing left but remnants of the desperation in your glossed-over eyes as you beg for mercy in those final seconds of your life."

His smile turned cold when he reached me, and his gold rings flashed again as they flitted in the air, his eyes lighting up as if he'd had a great epiphany. "Better yet, there are so many wonderful games we can play before we make it to that main event. Vivienne and I had such fun before I tore her throat open."

Cupping his chin thoughtfully, he pouted, and any remaining composure I maintained dropped from my shoulders and plummeted into my gut. The mere thought of Vivienne suffering before such a gruesome death sent a wave of nausea rolling through my stomach.

"Mind-compulsion magic is a beautiful thing!" he said. "Committing unspeakable acts against your own flesh, against your will … well, there are worse things than death, yes?"

Before anyone could respond to his command and sickening admission, his thoughts penetrated mine when he stepped closer to meet my face, his hot breath warm on my lips, eyes once again lowering to my necklace as he sent me his thoughts.

Do I have your attention, Camille? He trailed a finger over my chest, strengthening the fireball as it fluttered inside of me. The searing pain vibrated through my ribcage and I cringed, unable to buckle over since his power held me upright. His finger trailed lightly down my torso, lower and lower, until his hand slipped between my legs and possessively gripped the inside of my thigh. Every muscle south of my waistline clenched and I whimpered at the overwhelming sensation of arousal he created; a repulsive blend of pleasure and pain wracked my body. I tried to extinguish my desire for him, but my effort met futility. He grinned down at me, the heel of his hand rubbing slow circles into my thigh, the sensation a volcanic bubble on the verge of eruption.

Compulsion is a beautiful thing , he said, teasing me to the height of climax, the need for release excruciating, *and there are some things worse than death.*

Gavin and Arianna's yelling was muffled in the distance, but all I could focus on was Gérard's seductive speech in my head and the unbearable torture he was inflicting on my body. Just as I was about to fall apart in ecstasy beneath his touch, he removed his hand from my legs and denied me the release, forcing me to cry out in humiliating protest. He ignored my cry and continued to send me his thoughts. *Gavin might be the leader in this mission to destroy me, but you are the firestarter. Think twice about what knowledge you choose to divulge in your efforts to save everyone. It just might be the very knowledge that destroys you all.*

With that, the burning in my chest ceased, my arousal dissipated, and Gérard, sucking his fingers, turned on his heel to retreat down the staircase, over Marie's body, and out the front door, where he vanished among the trees.

3

PURPOSE

A light tingling itched my right hip over my crescent scar. The soft brushing stirred me from my haze.

"*Mmmmm* ," I opened my eyes, my lashes fluttering against the soft sunlight that poured in from the living room blinds.

"*Ssshhh* , easy, love." Gavin's soothing voice called my attention upward, where he stood hovering over me as I lay on the sofa. He peered down with hungry eyes, his fingers grazing the scar, smoothing his thumb and forefinger over it and across my hipbone. "He drained your energy and you passed out. You're safe now."

"Drained me ... what?" I met his fingers with mine, linking them. "But I'm not human."

"It's Gérard. He drains whomever he pleases." Undoing the link I created, he pulled his fingers away and leaned down on his knees to kiss the scar, letting his lips linger over my hip. Desire flamed beneath the spot his mouth touched and my grogginess began to dissipate. I squirmed under him, a small smile springing to his lips when he heard my soft moan. Sliding on top of me, he gently aligned his body with mine, the heat in his eyes making my breath jump. "Seeing him walk up to you like that, seeing him touch you ..." He bent down and drew the skin of my neck into his mouth, sucking softly. "I thought I might lose you for good and there wasn't a damn thing I could do about it. It was the most helpless, terrifying feeling." He leaned on an elbow and pulled his shirt over his head, tossing it to the floor, his gaze a liquid fire, still trained on mine. "Are you all right? What did he do to you?" His mouth found my neck again, more urgent this time, brushing wet kisses up to my ear and down over my collarbone.

The image of Gérard's greedy, malevolent eyes as they bored into mine, the way his hand gripped my thigh as if he owned it, made my eyes squeeze shut in disgust. Worse yet, the way he violated me, paralyzing me with desire, made my stomach turn. I needed Gavin's hands on me. Only his.

"Gav, I need you to be inside of me," I whispered, opening my eyes.

He searched my face for any sign of distress and must have seen the panic, because he stilled and ran his thumb along the line of my jaw as if to console me.

"Cam, I don't know if—"

"Gavin, please." I squeezed his shoulders, implored him with my gaze.

After a beat, he gently eased down my jeans zipper, ridding me of the fabric between us before nudging my legs open. My body arched into him and he groaned, freeing himself before hooking his thumbs into the sides of my panties and sliding them down. The house was quiet except for our soft panting, and as he bared my skin, memories of the encounter with Gérard slipped away. Screwing his eyes tight as he entered me, he hissed through his teeth and his jaw fell slack, a low gasp escaping when he eased farther in. My arms fell over his shoulders, my fingers digging into them to encourage his slow, rocking rhythm.

"Promise me whatever happens, we stick together, no matter what," I whispered.

Our mouths met and his teeth locked onto my lower lip before his tongue caressed the upper one. Burying his hands into my hair as he moved, he nodded, his eyes filled with intense promise. I shivered at the sensations he sent through my body, the feel of his taut shoulder muscles contracting beneath my fingertips, his grip desperate and hips determined as he dipped them between my thighs.

"No matter what," I repeated, my voice thick with need, breath quickening as he increased his rhythm. That felt … oh, God. That felt good.

"We're one, no matter what. You have my word," he smoothed one hand down my side and over my hip, settling on my upper thigh to hitch it higher. My head rolled back and my moans dissolved into soft mewls, coaxing a guttural growl from his chest, causing him to slam harder into me, his breath catching, resulting in the sexiest sounds I'd ever heard come from a man in my life. Hearing them was my undoing.

The steady rocking pace he'd begun evolved into a frenzied wave of sharp thrusts, pushing us both further and further into a paradisiacal state, kneading each other's skin and devouring one another's mouths with carnal abandon. Gavin cried out against my lips and I followed him. The sound of something falling, then scattering onto the hallway floor, broke through the incoherent sounds of our orgasms.

"Oh, dear God!" Audrey's voice sputtered from the hall. Our heads snapped in her direction and we both winced when Gabe bumped into her from behind, not looking where he was going, preoccupied with his iPod. She shrieked and Gabe jumped back, eyeing the broken plates around their feet with confusion. Then his chin shot up and he spotted Gavin and me on the couch.

"*Bahahaha!*"

"Gabriel!" Audrey bumped him with her elbow and covered his eyes, keeping hers wide open. "For crying out loud! This is the quietest you two have ever been, I had no idea you were in here!"

Quiet? Funny. I thought nukes dropped around us and the room imploded while our bodies burst to flame. Perspective is a funny thing.

"Here I am baking cookies and looking all over the house for *you*," she turned her attention to Gabe and uncovered his eyes, "hoping to bring my man something to munch on, and instead I walk in on *your* crazy monkey sex! Thanks you two, now I'm officially scarred for life." She swatted the air in front of her, as if she could shoo away the images, and darted over the broken dishes and cookies, up the staircase, with a flustered string of expletives.

Gabe watched her ascend the stairway and let out another amused cackle. "Oh don't mind her. She's acting like she just witnessed her parents in the act." Bending down, he snatched a cookie and gave us a thumbs-up. "You look hot, kids. Carry on."

He jogged up the stairs after her, shouting with a mouth full, "Cookies, babe? Marie just died, and you're baking cookies?"

"Baking is how I handle grief!" she shouted back.

"Who are you, Paula Deen?"

A door slammed, and that was the end of that conversation.

Gavin and I erupted into laughter, rushing to sit up and cover ourselves. Pinching his thumb in his zipper, Gavin yelped. "*Ow*, damn!" His quiet chuckle made me smile even wider and my eyes met his, locking on target. His lashes fluttered as he blinked, holding my stare with equal adoration, removing his thumb from his lips to lean down and burn me with a kiss. His hands cupped over the hair around my ears; he pressed his forehead to mine. "No matter what," he whispered.

"We're one."

"Cam?"

"*Hhhmm?*"

He paused.

"Are you going to tell me what happened with Gérard earlier, when he walked up to you?"

Do I have your attention Camille? I swallowed and blinked, recalling the heat from Gérard's revolting touch and thoughts.

"Nothing. He just tried to scare me. And it worked."

***

The sun had begun to set while I parked myself at a cafe table on the cozy streets of downtown Breaux Bridge, wanting to surround myself with the memories of my small town life, even for just a moment. Although I had spent most of my time working and going to school in Lafayette, people still knew me in the Breaux Bridge area, since I lived here. It was risky to be out in the open like this, so close to Lafayette and the countless missing person's flyers that littered its streets. But I needed a breather. After Gérard's visit, the mood in the house tanked even further when Gavin and Gabe decided to take Marie's body to London, to bury her near Joel's old home. While they were there, they had some last-minute preparations to make with other members of the resistance, so I decided to spend our last night on earth in my old hometown.

I kept my nose buried behind a book, peeking out through massive sunglasses to people watch as the locals strolled by. My beanie hat covered most of my hair, and I pulled it loosely over my ears with the hopes of being more inconspicuous. I shut my eyes while I thought of poor Marie, and sipped my tasteless cafe macchiato. Even loaded up with tons of caramel, it did nothing for my vampire taste buds. But it made me look the part, so I continued to suck it down.

Marie. *Gone.* The same Marie that I'd mentally vowed to protect just hours ago. Marie, Arianna's final link to her deceased best friend and lover, Joel. *Gone*, because of this mess. Because of me and what I'd caused. No matter what Gavin said, his whole mission never would have been sidelined and rerouted like this if it weren't for me barging into Amaranth after Gavin like some lovesick, impulsive girl. I had no idea what I was really getting myself into, not to mention what I was dragging my best friends, my family, into because of it.

Swallowing hard, I fished a cigarette from my pocket. Now was not the time to dwell on what I couldn't go back and change. It was time to own my choices and move on, damn the consequences. My mother's words came back to haunt me, suddenly fitting and poignant given our current situation. *Once you know something, you can never unknow it. Truth doesn't let you do that. That's the tragedy of knowledge.'* I knew the weight of my decisions and what they meant for all of us now, and I'd never be able to undo that knowledge.

A light breeze brushed the back of my shoulder as I lit up and I froze in my seat, but then relaxed when Arianna slid into the seat across from me.

"Jumpy much?" She smiled, sliding her sunglasses

over her head.

"Can you blame me?"

"Guess not. What are you doing out here all by yourself? Homesick?"

"A little. It's hard to imagine I ever lived here. That I hung out on these streets, shopped at these stores. That was my favorite lunch place," I pointed to the terracotta orange brick building across the street. The dark green wrought-iron railing formed a quaint walkway, the doors and windows decked out in Parisian-themed, hand-painted signs. "They made a mean shrimp po'boy."

"I know it's a lot to leave behind." She eyed the restaurant with a sad smile. "I've started over so many times, I've kind of become immune to that sentimentality. The attachment to things, I mean."

"I'm sorry, that must be hard. Especially after … you know, after Joel."

"Thanks." She looked down, twirled a long golden lock around her finger. "Losing him was certainly the most painful adjustment I'd had to make in my lifetime. Although I don't know if it was the hardest."

"What do you mean?"

"I think losing my humanity has been the hardest. All the back and forth over the years, turning from human to vampire and back again. It's been exhausting. Adjusting to the loss of the small things you take for granted as a human, like the feel of the rain on your skin, or the way sweet tea tastes on a really hot day. Simple pleasures that just aren't the same when you're a frozen soul. When

I left Amaranth during the uprising, I was certain I'd remain human when I returned to earth, that I would never let anything else convince me to turn again. It was a fresh start."

"Why did you?" I'd wanted to know this since I first met Arianna, wanted to understand why she'd turned vampire again after escaping Amaranth during the uprising in the 1800s: why she didn't hang on to her humanity while she had the chance. Then again, had she done that, she'd be long gone by now and I would have never had the privilege to meet her. She was lovely, loyal, and pure, and I strived to possess strength like hers someday. As sad as I was for her frozen state, I was happy to have her in my life.

"Why didn't I remain human? Gavin," she answered, meeting my gaze. "When I returned to earth, and he'd found out his parents were killed after the uprising died down, found out how Samira used them, he was enraged. He had his mind made up then. He'd change and organize a rebellion, plan a course of attack and bring Samira down. That mission evolved, eventually turning into something bigger than avenging his parents' death. As he traveled the world and met more frozen souls, he wanted to save them, too. He wanted to save everyone," she let out a soft laugh, glancing toward the sunset. "There was no stopping him then, and Gabe and Josh, loyal mates as they were, vowed to help him. They made a pact to remain brothers till the end, hell or high water. Joel joined them—he was already a vampire at the time—and it took many years for them to make progress with other frozen souls, to recruit them and hatch a plan for a resistance movement. Anyway, when I found the three of them changed, I was devastated, because I knew."

She shook her head with certainty, releasing a heavy sigh. "I knew I might never see my brother human again. And I couldn't bear it, couldn't grow old knowing he'd remain cursed on earth. Especially when I knew all of this was a result of my mother and her kingdom. So, I had Gavin change me into a vampire again."

"I can't believe he hasn't told me this." My brows pulled together and I reached over to place my hand on hers, squeezed her knuckles tightly. "That's the most selfless thing I've ever heard."

"It's crazy the things we do when we want to protect the ones we love."

Lowering my eyes to our locked hands, I slowly pulled away to lean back in my seat.

"Camille, I know you want to protect my brother. I know you want to help all of us. But you have to know that whatever is going on with these visions, and whatever my father said to you, you have to tell us what you know."

"I don't know anything."

"You're good at many things. Lying is not one of them."

"Ari, I'm not lying to you. I don't know … what he meant."

"So he did say something to you?"

"He warned me. That was it, I promise." I wouldn't dare confess what else her father had done to me.

"Warned you about what?"

I bristled in my chair, unable to meet her intent gaze, unsure how to answer. What did Gérard's warning really mean, anyway? *Think twice about what knowledge you choose to divulge in your efforts to save everyone.* Why couldn't I decode it? What the hell was he talking about? What knowledge? He spoke to me as if I knew, but I was more lost than ever.

"He just told me to be careful about what I choose to tell you guys in order to save you. But I have no idea what he meant by that."

Arianna's eyes narrowed and she sat back, taking my words in. My gaze settled past her shoulders, on a little boy at the end of the sidewalk. He was wandering toward us, tears pricking his eyes as he twisted his fingers and glanced around, his soft sobs intensifying with each step that brought him closer and closer to our table. Arianna shifted to find the source of the crying, and my heart lurched in my chest when he locked eyes with me.

His big blue irises were filled with fear, his breathing rapid and heart rate thumping so heavily I could feel it in my own chest. He held my gaze and paused for a beat, taking tentative steps toward me when I didn't look away. Instantly anxious, I rose to my feet and waited.

He approached me and reached out to grip onto my finger with one little pinky, latching on and staring up at me, pleading.

Bending down to meet him at eye level, I let him grasp harder at my finger, his worry transferring and imprinting on me, causing tears to spring up in my own eyes. A faint stinging sensation attacked my temples and I flinched.

"Cam?" Arianna stood from her seat and bent down to face us.

Everything became clear. Our skin-to-skin link giving me a direct hotline to the little boy's worries. "He's terrified." The words were automatic, my eyes unblinking and glued to his. "He's lost his mom, hasn't seen her in thirty minutes. The last place he remembers seeing her is the blue flower shop three blocks up the road, the one with iris and lily arrangements in the front window. But the shop's closed now. He's too afraid to ask an adult for help because he doesn't like strangers."

The words rushed from my lips and the tears chased them. Arianna's eyes widened as I stood. Taking the boy by the hand, I patted it gently. "It's okay, buddy. Let's go inside this shop here and make a phone call to find your mommy."

He buried his head into the crook between my arm and leg, allowing me to lead him into the shop. I gave Arianna a nod before entering, leaving her standing there, staring curiously at the little boy's hand in mine.

***

"Camille?" Gavin's voice was faint, but I recognized

this feeling. It was breaking through, penetrating the outer haze that always surrounded me like a smothering bubble whenever I slipped off into the dream state, when I saw the visions. He and Gabe must've returned from their business in London. *How long have I been out this time?*

"She's coming out of it, give her a second," Arianna's voice replied, getting clearer with each syllable. Next came Gabe and Audrey's voices, but I couldn't quite make the sentences out. Just when I thought I was about to snap out of it, a thick ripple roped me back into the bubble, bombarding me with images of a dark, fog-filled bayou, Gavin and me sitting in an old, baby-blue rowboat, headed toward a destination with flashlights in hand. Our faces were focused, our time was short.

And then my heart swelled with hope at the sound of Vivienne's voice. *Take the south end of the Bayou Teche nah, child. You'll know what to do, ya hear? Hurry nah, before it's too late. Before it's too late, before it's too late, before ...*

As her voice trailed off, the vision blurred and my friends' voices grew louder, clearer, until the bubble popped and I found Arianna softly shaking my shoulder. My eyes immediately zoned in on the Book of the Ancients on top of Gavin's piano, and I stood from the couch to move toward it, gently breaking through my circle of friends. They all turned to watch me like a circus animal about to do another trick. Had I not been so focused on the damn book, it might have been amusing and given me a good laugh.

"Unbelievable," Audrey's voice squeaked as I pushed past her. "Here we are, talking to you about your freaky little-boy encounter back in Breaux Bridge and how your caramel macchiato tasted like cardboard, and boom! You just zone out like one of the kids from *Children of the Corn*."

"Um, Aud, babe … I don't think those kids zone out. They're just freaky twenty-four-seven. It's a year-round thing." Gabe's response drew a half-hearted laugh from me, but it was quickly reined in when I reached the Book of the Ancients.

"Whatever, Gabriel," Audrey said to him. "My point is, it's freaky, okay? She gets this glazed-over look in her eyes, like she's gonna whip out a butcher knife and go all Michael Myers on us or something."

I glanced over my shoulder to cock an eyebrow at her.

"Oh, *now* you pay attention." She cocked an eyebrow back.

"What is it with you and the cheesy horror-movie references?" Gabe muttered.

"Hey, now. *Halloween* is a classic," Gavin scolded him. "Don't go hating on the classics."

Audrey shushed them both and came to join me at the piano. "Well? Are you just going to stand there and stare at it? What is it?"

I blinked, recalling the one thing that had stuck out in this new vision. Aside from the fact that Gavin and I were in a rowboat, in a part of the bayou I'd never seen before, I'd noticed the Book of the Ancients was propped on my lap as Gavin rowed. I shut my eyes as if to replay the scene in my mind, opening them when I realized I couldn't summon the vision back.

But I knew. The book, *this* book, was with us in the boat.

The cover slammed open in front of me. The gust of wind caused our little gathering to stumble backward. The pages flipped as it blew open, landing on the empty pages near the back.

"*Okayyyy ...* " Gabe stepped back with his hands up.

"Holy *Poltergeist.*" Audrey's voice came alive with awe, and she pushed the hair out of her eyes.

Sliding the book toward me, I rested my elbows on the piano lid and turned the empty pages, a zap of energy pinning my attention to one of the last blank pages. Skimming my fingers over the parchment, beautiful gold trails of light followed my fingertips, gliding, twisting, and turning, illustrating and illuminating a path of arrows. The page continued to come alive with each trace of my fingers, the golden light beaming upward and onto our faces, the image more vivid as the light grew in intensity.

"It's a map," I said, examining each path and waterway that appeared, taking in the lush foliage that surrounded it, springing up from the page like a three-dimensional picture book.

"What's that in the waterway?" Gavin asked, leaning over my shoulder to get a better look.

"It's my vision," I whispered in realization, studying the light as it shaped an outline of a small boat with oars attached to the side. The oars began to move, the motion pushing the picture of the boat along, up the waterway toward a small shack on the bank, Vivienne's voice echoing in my head. *Take the south end of the Bayou Teche nah, child. You'll know what to do, ya hear?*

I blinked and turned to look at my friends, just to make sure I wasn't falling into another trance. *Hurry nah, before it's too late. Before it's too late, before it's too late, before …*

"Before it's too late," I whispered.

"Huh?" Gavin glanced between me and the illustration. "Too late for what?"

"I have to go here, wherever this is. Before it's too late … before we leave for Amaranth tomorrow." As soon as the words were off my tongue, the golden light disappeared and the map faded, the book slamming shut.

Just like that, I had my answer.

And never before had an answer confused me more. Answers were supposed to give you peace, give you some kind of direction. Instead, this one was leading me further into the darkness, encouraging me forward onto a path I wasn't sure I wanted to take. I couldn't even see the steps in front of me, only the signs.

I scooped up the Book of the Ancients and grabbed Gavin's hand, and led him past our friends, out of the house, and into the night.

4

HAUNTED

The setting sun dressed the bayou's horizon in a sultry, lazy glow, the bank's trees casting dramatic shadows over the water. Gavin and I approached the southern part of the Teche that was shown to me in my vision.

He caught my arm as we neared the edge of the bank. "Come on, love. We don't really need to search by boat. Let's take to the trees and search that way."

"No," I murmured, glancing around. "The vision was very specific, we have to go by boat." We'd fueled up on blood, and we'd run all the way here, occasionally dipping into flight amongst the trees. It helped to burn off some of my pent-up energy, but slowing down to look around and figure out the next step felt frustrating. The Book of the Ancients was stowed in a backpack over my shoulder, and all I could think about was where to find this baby-blue rowboat so we could bring my vision to life.

Why it had to be exactly as my vision, I didn't know. All I knew was that I was compelled to mimic it, traveling the waterways by rowboat, a specific rowboat. It was a feeling just as sure as the certainty I'd felt when the little boy wandered up to me on the street. I knew he needed help, and in that instant, it was my sole purpose to help him find his way to his mom. If I didn't complete that task, I would have been broken, a mechanical malfunction that needed a missing part to operate properly again.

And that surety fueled my direction now.

Gavin shot me an apprehensive side-glance and then stationed himself beside me, slipping his hands in his pockets. "Well, I don't think a blue rowboat is going to appear out of thin air. And flying would get us to wherever we need to go faster. Do you remember anything else?"

I bit the inside of my lip and turned in a slow circle, letting my eyes study our surroundings. "Nothing comes to mind, but this is where we're supposed to start searching."

"Well ..." His voice was unconvinced. "Let's start heading up the bank, then, and go from there."

I nodded and trailed behind him, aware the darkness was imminent, the sunset almost complete. It was nightfall in my vision, the bayou enveloped in an eerie white fog that blanketed the water's surface and slithered through the surrounding trees. We walked farther north and within minutes, the sunlight was gone and our flashlights were on. Low croaks, high-pitched chirps, and soft cooing echoed all around us, the bayou's atmosphere swallowing us up in its hypnotic cocoon.

Twigs and leaves crunched beneath our feet, and Gavin stopped, swinging around to meet me.

"Baby, I don't know if—"

"*Sshhh* ," I lifted my head to the trees, then spun around when an echo of sinister laughter washed over me. "Do you hear that?"

His eyes widened and he withdrew his silver dagger, tucking me behind him. "Hear what? What is it?" His voice dropped low and husky, his jaw set.

"Cammmmillle," the voice hissed, followed by more laughter, and I withdrew my own blade, readying my stance while my eyes bounced everywhere to locate the source. I stumbled and bumped into Gavin when I heard another echo of poisonous snickering, the seductive, velvet sound sliding through me, making the hairs on my neck erect.

"You really don't hear that?"

"Hear what? All I hear is insects and alligators."

I straightened and planted my feet into the muddy ground, shutting my eyes with hopes of pushing the voice out, away from us, out of my head, which is where I suspected it was originating in the first place.

Good God, I was really losing it.

My lashes flittering as I blinked, I reopened my eyes and flew back, smacking into Gavin's chest. He wrapped his arms around me in a protective hold. Amidst the inky backdrop of the nearby bushes, beneath the ghoulish overlay of stringy Spanish moss, Scarlet snaked around the branches, weaving in and out of the oaks in a vibrant, apple-red silk dress, the thin spaghetti straps hugging her luminous white skin while the flowing skirt swayed around her knees.

"Scarlet," I choked, pushing back farther against Gavin's chest. He tightened his grip around me and I could feel his chin move above my head, searching for the vixen in red.

"Where?" He spoke low and hushed, shifting us to the left, then to the right. "Cam, hurry, tell me where she is."

"Right there." I followed her with my eyes as she held my gaze and frolicked between two gigantic oaks.

"Cammmilllle," she cooed again, this time breaking eye contact with me to prance farther back into a copse of trees. The branches and moss seemed to entangle her entire form, reaching and wrapping around her arms and legs as she moved, but she showed no sign of distress, only a smirk. Her fingers toyed with the moss as it caressed her skin, eyes dancing with delight as it slithered beneath her long chestnut locks. She was an angelic serpent, a deceitful goddess of nature. When her eyes locked with mine again, the image stole my breath away.

"Gavin, right there!" I pointed to the space between the oaks, gulping hard when she continued to slink in and around the brush, her body starting to fade in and out before my eyes. Her arms and legs were suddenly flickering as they worked in slow motion. "How do you not see her? She's right there!" As she faded in and out, I darted toward her, afraid I might lose sight of her.

As I moved forward, I tried to shake my head from the spell, from the ensnaring trap of her beauty. If I wasn't careful, I'd let her lead us deep into the bayou, where who knew what awaited us. If we lifted off into flight, if we flew out of the bayou to escape, other troubles would ensue. What kind of troubles, I hadn't a clue. But my gut told me to steer clear of the skies above this part of the Teche.

It struck me then that this could be a trick, that it could be Gérard luring us into danger somehow. Unconvinced of that theory, though, I continued to trudge forward into the brush, my gaze still glued to Scarlet's faint form.

Gavin's voice echoed distantly from behind, and he lassoed me backward against him. When I turned with wild eyes to question him, his were just as wild. "Cam," he blinked and exchanged glances with me and the woods before us. His voice was clearer now. "No one is there, baby. There's … nothing there."

Frantic, determined to prove my sanity, I whipped my head back in the other direction and broke free from his hold, making a dash for the final glimpse of the luscious red of her dress. "This way, Gav. I have to follow her."

"Camille, stop it!" He was hot on my trail. "You're seeing things! Even if she was here, following her is a bad idea, now stop!" Reaching once more for my elbow, he latched on but I lurched forward, yanking him with me, surprised by my own strength. He must've been surprised too, because he nicked my forearm with his blade, with just the tip: just enough to provoke a hiss from my teeth and a small cloud of smoke to radiate from the scorched piece of skin. The effect threw me into whiplash and I swung around to face him, shocked that he'd cut me.

"What the hell are you doing?" I jerked my arm away, near feral at the idea of losing Scarlet's trail.

"No, what are *you* doing? We're going back and we're getting the hell out of here, Camille. Right the hell *now*. I don't know what's happening to you, but these visions … they're getting worse. And we don't need to be out here alone any longer than we have to." He shot me a fierce glare and held out his hand.

"But the boat—"

"There is no damn boat! And if there is, we're not going to bury ourselves deep in the swamp to find it when Gérard could be anywhere. Now let's go. And we're flying out of here, because none of this feels right." Grabbing my hand, he wrapped me against him and prepared to launch us into flight, but something foreign possessed me to take hold of my knife and nick him back. His eyes flew wide in shock when the silver sliced the skin of his forearm.

The next few seconds were downright terrifying, because I didn't know what came over me. I began to fight him.

My arms shot up and he quickly chopped at my wrist to break the dagger from my hand, letting out a whoosh of air when I planted my boot-clad foot into his midsection.

"Camille!" he barked through gritted teeth, his reflexes fast. His grip locked onto my calf and he spun me up off the ground and into midair, at the same time knocking the knife from my hand with ease. My mind screamed to stop, to quit resisting him, but my body was in charge. He needed to let me go after Scarlet. I needed him to back off—no matter what it took to show him that.

A bug being spun into a spider's web, I twirled in the air at rapid speed, yielding to his direction.

Until his hand left my calf for a split second.

Flipping backward and landing on two feet, I lurched backward and ricocheted off the side of a tree trunk to give myself leverage to charge him. Once again, he was too fast, ducking and darting to the left when I shot toward him like a cannon. He cursed under his breath and I slid across the dirt to reach down and grab my knife again. Leaping forward to beat me to the weapon, his boots kicked dirt in his wake and we slammed into one another.

"No!" My voice was vicious, completely unrecognizable. "We have to keep going." My fingers curled around the dagger, and I summoned every ounce of power within me to shove myself into him and force us both upward and backward, until he was pinned against the same tree I'd used to charge him. My knife to his throat, our chests heaving, I realized he wasn't fighting my grip on him. Instead, his eyes lowered to the knife, widening a fraction at the sound of the low growl that emitted from my throat.

"Camille, it's me, Gavin. Your husband. I know you're in there."

Just like that, the force that had taken my body hostage was gone, and I staggered back, sliding the dagger back into my belt sleeve. "I saw Scarlet ... or something that resembled her ... and I'm going after her whether you like it or not." Though weak and panting, my voice had returned along with my free will.

Keeping his back to the tree and his intense gaze on me, he reached out and leaned forward to swipe a thumb over my cheek. The gentle gesture caused me to exhale and lean into his palm.

"Something isn't right, baby," he said. "I don't like this."

"I promise we'll fly up and out of here the second something else feels off. You have my word."

"I don't know if it'll be much good if you pull another Linda Blair on me."

I felt the anxious lines on my face soften into a small smile at yet another cheesy horror-movie reference. First Audrey, and now my Hitchcock fan-boy husband. He returned my smile with a relieved grin, letting me take him by the hand. I started in the general direction I'd last seen the vision of Scarlet, shuffling forward through the thickets of sticks, mud and branches, stopping abruptly when we rounded a group of trees to find a nestled, off-the-beaten waterway, broken apart from the main bank, and what did you know …

A baby-blue rowboat.

"Cam, if Scarlet is the one who led us here … this could still be dangerous."

"Gav, this was the boat in my vision. This is right. I promise you, please trust me."

"It's not you I don't trust. It's these visions … this *thing*, whatever's taking over you."

"You saw the map in the Book of the Ancients with your own two eyes. Vivienne's book. How dangerous can the vision be if it matched what the book showed us?"

"The witches and frozen souls are enemies. We can't necessarily trust everything the witches' book shows us." Threading his fingers through mine, his gaze flicked up and from side to side, monitoring our surroundings.

"Well, we saw what happened with the prophecies in Amaranth, and we've been following Vivienne's guidance even before that, so there's no reason to stop now. We mean the witches no harm, and we can prove that if need be. Now come on." I tugged him with me and stepped into the boat, Gavin and me sitting opposite one another, just as I saw in my vision.

Pulling the Book of the Ancients from my bag and placing it on my lap, I kept my flashlight in hand and watched carefully as Gavin began to row. The fact that Scarlet—or a whacked-out hallucination of her—had led us to this boat was definitely discomforting, but I trusted the book on my lap, trusted what it had shown us just this evening. I only prayed that wherever the boat was taking us, it would be a safe place. And that it would lead to answers.

Yeah. Answers would be really good right about now, considering the fact that I just attacked my own husband.

Floating quietly across the waterway, the fog surrounding us became more and more disorienting, our flashlights only adding to the feeling of strangeness. The wider part of the bayou seemed to disappear; the off-beaten path we were on had been immersed in the swamp's watery maze. We weren't getting anywhere, it seemed, and it felt like we'd been rowing for hours. Gavin and I didn't speak, and glided along in silence while I flipped open the Book of the Ancients every few minutes, waiting for it to miraculously light up again or … something.

"Come on, damn it." I slammed it shut for the thousandth time, looking out into the creepy fog that covered us like a quilt. I thought of pulling my cell from my backpack to check the time, but decided against it when I figured I'd get no reception. It probably wouldn't even turn on. I couldn't remember the last time I charged it, and found myself barely caring. It was about that time— time to feed.

"Getting hungry?" Gavin asked.

"Did you just … read my thoughts?"

"*Haha* , no, love. I can't read your thoughts until you develop the ability to read our coven's, and only if you let me break through *their* barrier so I can tune in. But it's got to be getting close to midnight, because I'm starved, too. And your eyes are going gray."

Now that he'd mentioned food, I wanted more than food; I wanted to hunt. Even though we didn't technically hunt and kill, the desire was still there. I could feel my eyes shift hard and black at the thought of sinking my fangs into warm blood. Warm skin. Soft flesh …

Quivering, I nodded. "Yeah, but it can wait."

"I think it might have to. Had I known we'd be gone this long, I would have brought something."

"We don't even know where we are. I don't recognize a damn thing. If this book doesn't light up like a Christmas tree again soon, I say we ditch this and head home."

He let out a soft chuckle. "That's just the hunger talking. You nearly took me out back there, just to get me in this boat. We're going to keep at it until we find what we're looking for."

The witches, the magic, my freaky new sixth sense—something—must've heard Gavin's words, because the fog began to thin out behind him, revealing the tiny wood shack from my vision, lit aglow by a single lantern in the grime-covered front window.

"There! Behind you." Excited, I shifted my body and stood, nearly tipping us.

"Easy, love," he worked to steady us. "Okay, let's get this show on the road." Veering off toward the patch of solid ground, he ran the edge of the rowboat aground and helped me out.

With the help of only our flashlights and the dim lantern light glowing from the shack's window, we approached the filthy, weathered door and knocked. Familiar blue cobalt glass hung from the trees, and the same brick dust from Vivienne's old shop lined the windowsill and doorway. Knowing none of it would have any effect on us because we were frozen souls, I decided to speak up and inform whoever was inside of our intentions, so we didn't appear a threat.

"Hello?" I called out, waiting before I knocked again. "We don't mean to bother you, but we really need your help. My name's Camille and I've—"

"Seen this in one of your visions?" The shaky, tired voice greeted me as the door opened a crack. A short elderly woman with brittle white hair appeared, her face so wrinkled it made it hard to see where her eyelids began and ended. Her thin, dry lips were set in a grim, straight line, and her glassy eyes found mine as she looked up at me, lighting the space between us with the candle in her hand. Shrouded in a navy blue dress that looked like a potato sack, the woman was adorned in jewelry made of the earth. Her mouth slightly worked, as if she was chewing nonstop on straw. Once she opened her mouth to speak again and I saw her teeth, I thought maybe it was tobacco she'd been chewing.

"I said, you seen this here place in your visions?"

"Oh, yes, ma'am. You ... know about them?"

"*Yess* , *yesss*, come in, come in."

She opened the door wider and led Gavin and me

inside, without so much as a word about us being frozen souls. The thought comforted me. It must have meant she was expecting us, or at least knew we didn't mean her harm. Silver daggers, similar to ours, sat on a small wooden table, perhaps her only defense from frozen souls since her magic was of no use against them. I gave them a discreet glance, drawing even more comfort from the fact that she didn't seem interested in reaching for one to protect herself.

"*Mmm*," she turned to face Gavin once we were inside. "*Yesss*, here. This is him, ain't it Viv?"

My heart leaped in my chest and Gavin's eyes found mine.

"Did you just say—?"

"*Nuh-uh*," the old woman grunted. "Viv's not *here*, she's here," she tapped her temple and nodded, lifting the candle closer to Gavin's face to get a good look. "The beginning of things to come, *eh*?"

"You talk to Vivienne?" My voice piped up at the thought of this woman being able to communicate with her. I wanted to ask a million questions, if that was the case. Too many questions. I held my tongue for a moment. "I mean, you can hear her? Or …"

"I can't hear her now, no." The woman gently poked Gavin's cheek with a weak, wrinkled finger. He just stared back at her, his gaze sliding to mine when she pulled back. "But we were linked, before she passed on. *Mmmm*. She sent you two to me. *Yesss*, right here."

Setting down the Book of the Ancients on her tiny

wood table, I crossed my arms. "I'm sorry, I'm not sure we know what you mean."

"Some of our kind creates links to one another. Whether because of friendship or ancestry, doesn't matter. When we create a link to one another, we just know we're tied. Can feel it, ya see. It's a, a means of communication for those we leave behind. Our link can act as a messenger, carry on information after we're gone. Vivienne linked herself to me right before she went. Before *he* came for her."

"Before he came … you mean the man who killed her?" Gavin stuck his hands in his pockets, the floor creaking under his weight when he shifted.

"*Piisshhh* ," the woman batted her hands in dismissal, wobbled over to the small stove where a teakettle hissed steam. "If that's what you want to call him. An abomination is what he is, a murderer is more like it. *Mmm, yesss.* She linked me to her right before he killed her, gave me some news about your … situation. Something private."

"Really?" I stepped forward and one of the silver knives flew off the table and toward her hand. Her fragile fingers grasped it, her cloudy eyes locking with mine. I raised my hands and stepped back.

"Not everyone enjoys being linked, you see. It can mean bad things for the receiver."

"Ma'am … I don't expect you to believe anything a frozen soul tells you, but we mean you no harm."

Gavin cleared his throat and nodded, agreeing with me. "Yes, you have our word."

"*Mmm* , that's all well and good boy, but it's not just you two I have to worry about. The messages Vivienne left me gave me no reason not to trust you, but it was clear that your situation revolves around your creator. And that's no good for me, now. I'm old as dirt but I'm not ready to pass on to the next world just yet."

As much as I understood this woman's concern, my patience was nearly gone. I wanted to know what crucial information Vivienne left for us. Why she'd gone through so much trouble to lure us here. "I understand being Vivienne's link must be a burden for you, and what happened to her … it was wrong … horrific. I know we can't make promises about what Gérard will or won't do after we leave your home, but we need this information. We—"

"*Mmm* ," the woman's voice hummed as she poured her hot water. "Slow down, slow, now. It's my job to tell you what I know. But first, you must realize that this is all written, but only your actions will determine if these things come to pass as they should. Fate is fate, but the outcomes can change, do you understand?"

Gavin and I exchanged glances. *Great. Talk about pressure.*

"The visions you've been having, they were sent to you by Vivienne right before she died. She knew she'd learned something dangerous. Which is why she linked herself to me and used the visions to communicate with you, so you'd find me. Aside from Viv, I'm one of the few original conjurers left in these parts. She was able to cast a spell on you, that would allow the visions to penetrate your thoughts, even in the event that you turned into a frozen soul, by tapping in to my power. A spell of that nature needed power from two originals, you see. A sort of permission from two parties in the same family, since it goes against our beliefs to be mixing and communicating with your kind. Plus, the natural immunity your kind has to our magic doesn't help none. And she was darn lucky I agreed. It's downright stupid for our kind to help yours learn how to use our magic. Gérard doesn't like the frozen souls knowing they have that power available to them, and when word starts getting around, he comes knocking on our doors with questions, you see. We start dying off. It's no wonder the last of our originals are living out in the middle of these no-good, godforsaken swamps!" She hissed the last words through her teeth and shook her head, dunking a tea bag into her mug as though she intended to crack the mug with her action.

"I know our kind has been … a nuisance to you." Gavin moved to stand beside me. "But we're trying to help, trying to end this. We want Gérard gone just as much as you do."

I eyed the tea bag as she beat it to a pulp with her spoon. "Ma'am—"

"The name's Clea."

"Clea. Okay. I started to see these visions right after I was changed. So that means—"

"It means those were Vivienne's final days. She knew

he was coming for her, and after she died, they grew stronger, yes?"

I nodded, reaching for a chair. "So what did she find that was so dangerous?" What could be more dangerous than deciding to help give us energy and protection for our trip to Amaranth? Wasn't she already in danger?

"She found the same thing you did. That Samira didn't hold the power to permanently lift the curse, and that killing her or draining Amaranth wouldn't be enough to destroy Gérard."

She paused, and I nodded, and Gavin did too.

"So, when she learned that, she discovered what would."

I was glad I was sitting down. Gavin reached out and clasped my hand at her words, and the news processed, hit me in the gut and sent my brain into overdrive, sending me up and out of my chair. "So there *is* a way to destroy him?" The possibility made every one of my cells tingle, made the hope rush over me in one massive tidal wave. And the memories. When we'd found out Samira was only the gatekeeper of Amaranth, only able to lift the vampire curse for those admitted into exile to feed Gérard's power, we'd hit a painful roadblock—that Gérard was who really held the key to lifting the curse for good. We'd known that he was the father of the frozen souls from the beginning, but Samira was the ruler, a hybrid just like him, with the ability to change vampires back into humans. The resistance was certain the answer to ending everything, including Gérard's power, was

Samira lifting the curse and draining Gérard's power source. When Samira told us the truth, that none of us would ever really be free until Gérard was destroyed, we weren't so sure if we could save everyone like we'd hoped.

But if Clea's words were true, really true, that changed everything.

"*Yess* , *yesss*," she answered, sipping her tea. "It all begins with the wolves, Dali and Akim."

5

IDENTITY

At the mention of Dali and Akim, I rose from the chair, cutting a glance at Gavin.

"We found something from Vivienne's shop," I said, returning my attention to Clea. "Something in her writing, about Dali and Akim. But we couldn't make out what it was."

Unsurprised, and equally unhurried by what I'd said, she continued to sip her tea, nodding as her thin lips bunched around the cup. "*Yesss, yesss.* Viv was on to the wolves. Gérard sensed this, just as he sensed the unrest brewing in Amaranth—the reason he came for her. The snake also confirmed this for him. She still lives."

"Scarlet," I whispered.

"*Mmmhmmm* , her roots go deep with your creator, *yesss.*" Her gaze slid to Gavin and he swallowed, breaking eye contact.

I couldn't ponder the meaning of that exchange right now. I had to know about the wolves. "Okay, so what about Dali and Akim?"

Setting her tea down, Clea stared at the mug for a moment before turning to step closer to Gavin and me. Her spicy scent carried through the air as her navy blue skirt swayed: a gypsy scent, worldly and ancient as dirt. She stood inches from us now, her wrinkly finger extending to stroke my chin. "The wolves, when turned back to their human state, are the key. The only thing that can destroy Gérard. You must convince Samira to lift the curse she placed on them and tell them that Vivienne sent you."

"Wait a minute, what?" Gavin moved closer. "Why on earth would we do that? Why would Samira agree to change them back? They are Gérard's original conjure mates. They wouldn't harm him, they'd help him. The last thing we need is two more conjurers with a lot of pent-up anger on the loose."

"Ah, you are a leader, but this is not the speech of a leader. Where is your instinct, my boy? The same that led you to the decisions that have brought you to this very spot?" Her finger left my chin and found his chest. "You must do this. You are the beginning, and your firestarter is by your side."

Her head tilted slightly, and my eyes flared at her description, the same description Gérard had given me.

"It is time to listen to those instincts once again," she said. "Put aside the logic and listen." Her finger dug deeper in to his chest and she burned him with those cloudy, distant eyes. "The things to come ... your role in the fate of your people ... all point to Dali and Akim.

Remove them from the equation, and you will fail the frozen souls."

I sucked in a sharp breath, her words from a moment ago still whirling in my mind. "What equation, Clea?"

"It is all written." Her reply bubbled up with a raspy cough and she stepped back. Whether she didn't hear my question or purposely ignored it, I didn't know. She resumed her tea drinking and settled into her rocking chair near the stove. "My link ends here, *yesss*, *yesss*. I've nothing else for you. Speak to Dali and Akim and you will know what to do."

Gavin nodded to me, turning for the door. "Thank you for your help, Clea."

"*Mmm , mmm.*" Her raspy voice was a murmur, her eyes set in a far-off haze. "Don't take to the skies in these parts, now. Gérard's magic blankets the trees here. He had it put there to prevent your kind from mingling with the original witches who live in these parts. If you fly, he'll know exactly where you are and that means trouble for us all. And it sounds to me you're already on his bad side. No need to go and make it worse, now."

Well, wasn't *that* the understatement of the century. It didn't matter that we had a legion of frozen souls on our side, a massive resistance movement: Gérard was still stronger. And we were indeed on his bad side.

I'd felt it in every bone in my body, in the way each hair stood on end when he drew his face so close, too close to mine. The pure terror that radiated from his presence when his eyes devoured my body told me an army of frozen souls meant nothing to him. He feared no frozen soul, only the ceasing of his power, of his personal destruction.

"Yes, thank you, Clea," I said, thankful I'd listened to my earlier instincts and not flown with Gavin through the swamp. Still quivering from these thoughts, I forced a tight smile, reaching for the Book of the Ancients. Clea's hand shot forward from her rocking chair, a streak of lightning staking its claim around my forearm. She latched on, her filmy eyes settling on my necklace, and Gavin was beside me in an instant, still and waiting.

My gaze dropped to the crescent moon locket and I winced, eyes snapping shut at the intensity of what was passing between us. My brow wrinkled as I focused, the sounds in the room overpowered when the visions came: me dashing up Samira's throne room stairs, grabbing Samira's hand and screaming something, every movement playing out in fragmented, choppy motion. Samira cried out as tears streamed down her face, both of us at once turning our attention to the center of the room, where ferocious, raging flames engulfed a group of faces that couldn't be made out.

My lips parted, releasing a loud gasp when my eyes shot back open. Clea's hand dropped gently to her lap, but she said nothing. Tears welled in my eyes and they grew heavy, instantly grieved by the sight of Samira's pain and the tears that betrayed her indifferent persona.

"Camille, it's time to go." Gavin spoke low through clenched teeth, hand on the small of my back. I grabbed the Book of the Ancients and he led me to the door. I glanced frantically over my shoulder, searching for answers in Clea's gaze, finding nothing but glassy pupils in a distant trance, the soft groaning of her rocking chair filling the room with eerie finality.

***

Gavin and I returned early in the morning from visiting Clea. The sun was just coming up when we decided to feed, and then fill Arianna in on our hurriedly decided plan to fly to Seattle, to visit my mom before our evening departure to the bayou portal. I'd put off a visit to my mother long enough, and if there was ever a time to try to make peace with her, now was that time.

Audrey and Gabe were asleep on the couch, wrapped together like a single pretzel in their matching striped PJs. "Ah, to be human again." Arianna glanced at them with a dramatic sigh. "But sleep is for wimps." She winked and kissed Gavin on the cheek, then squeezed me tight. "Be back by five. And refuel before you fly back, or such a long flight will be rough on your bodies before we go to Amaranth—"

"Sis," Gavin cocked a brow in her direction and eased the front door open, careful not to wake our human friends.

"Sorry, sorry. I'm totally turning into Audrey, aren't I?"

I pinched my fingers together, shrugging with a small smile. "We'll be as quick as we can, I promise. And we'll eat before we fly back, you have my word on that."

"*Mmmkay* . Love you two. Now hurry before the sleeping beauties wake."

Gavin and I flew into the early dawn, and part of me wished Gavin had listened to me and stayed behind in Louisiana. Sure, this last-minute trip across the country was a big deal right before we had to face Gérard, but I could've made it there and back on my own. Still, he wasn't having any of that, adamant that it was far too dangerous for me to be roaming around anywhere on my own, even if it was clear across the United States.

After kissing me on the doorstep of my mother's house, he disappeared around the corner, the wind of his wake blowing the long strands of my brown hair around my face. I took a deep breath and knocked, skipping the doorbell. My mother hated the doorbell. Said it was obnoxious.

The door creaked open and my mother's face appeared, eyes peering up at me in surprise from her wheelchair. She still wore her long, thin brown hair parted in the middle, the only change the strands of gray peeking through beneath the ashen Seattle sunlight. "Camille ..." An aging hand covered her mouth. "What are you doing here? You look ... different. Beautiful, but different."

"Hi, Mom. Thanks, can I ... come in?"

"Oh, uh ... of course, yes." She blinked and shook her head, wheeling herself backward to give me room. "The place is a mess, I can't believe you didn't tell me you'd be in town, it's been so long since you've—"

"Don't worry about it. And I know, I'm sorry I didn't call first. It was kind of a last-minute trip. And I can't stay long. I'm just in town to say hello and pick up some of Audrey's things."

"Audrey's things?"

"Yeah, she's living with me in Louisiana now. She moved out of her apartment here not long ago, and put some things into storage. I told her I'd go through some of her stuff while I came in town to visit you." Figuring the partial truth would suffice for an explanation of my random visit, I closed the door behind me and stepped into the gloomy living room. The television ran with the same *Godfather* movie my mom watched religiously ever since I was a kid. She probably knew it line by line by now.

Wading farther into the house, I let my eyes roam the fireplace mantel and coffee table, ashtrays and the same old pictures cluttering every corner and crevice. My shoulders falling at the sight, I thought, *This is what fear does to you. Freezes you in place.* My mother's isolated lifestyle was a product of giving up dreams, goals, and anything else that might have meant change. Even before she struggled with some of the limitations of her handicap, she'd stayed home and shut out the world, afraid to start over after the divorce, after her struggles with addiction. I'd always felt sympathy for her, for the fact that she'd allowed that fear to steal so much of her life, but the resentment still bubbled up when I saw her in person, when reminded of just how in denial she was of the need to move on, even after all this time.

But today was different.

It didn't matter that the house was exactly the same, that it was just as unkempt and cluttered as ever. There was a spark in her eyes, a life there I hadn't seen in … I didn't know how long. And that felt good to see in the flesh, especially after all this time. Relief pinged in my core, and I turned from the fireplace to face her.

"How are you, Mom? You look good."

"I do?"

"You do."

"I've been keeping up with my AA meetings, and seeing my therapist, you know." She glanced around sheepishly, her fingers knotted and fidgety on her lap. "I'm trying, Cam. I miss you terribly."

"I miss you, too."

"Can I get you something to eat or drink? I have coffee and leftovers from breakfast."

"No, thank you, though." I sat down on the loveseat, pushing aside a ratty newspaper.

"Your skin is glowing," Mom's eyes were gleaming, a soft smile in them. "It must be all of that Southern sunshine."

"Must be."

An awkward pause settled between us, *Godfather* dialogue the only sound filling the room.

"Camille, there's so much I've wanted to say to you, I don't know where to begin—"

"Me, too. But I want to start by saying I'm angry."

Before I could continue, the same uncomfortable burning sensation I'd experienced when I'd been lying on Samira's throne room floor, when I changed, seized my temples and I froze, wincing as I gripped my forehead. The mere mention of anger sent my mother into a mental flurry, and I could feel her anxiety escalating, seeping into my pores and fueling my own anxiety.

These random, fiery attacks were really starting to piss me off.

The burning strengthened when she wheeled closer to me and reached out to grasp my hand, but I managed to open my eyes and speak some more. "Just let me finish, don't worry. Don't worry, Mom," I grazed my fingers over her knuckles in a soothing rhythm and the burning lessened, the unease in her eyes softening. I sucked in a deep breath and swallowed, thankful for the relief. "I've been angry ... with myself, not you. I mean, I thought it was you I was angry with. And for a long time, I was, because of ... everything. But over these past few years, I've been angry with myself. For feeling responsible for taking care of you, for beating myself up for not being able to fix you." My voice cracked and I felt the tears coming, but I pushed them back, determined to finish what I came all this way to say. "None of that was my burden to bear, and I realize that now. Carrying all that weight only prevented me from moving on, and it probably left you with a lot of guilt. And the last thing I want is for you to feel guilt. I only want you to be at peace. That's important to me. Now more than ever."

Clasping my fingers tighter in hers, Mom's face tightened, throat visibly constricting when she let out a small spurt of air from her lips. She lowered her gaze to the couch cushions for a moment, then leveled it with mine again. "You don't know how much it means to me to hear that. These years of not speaking to you ..." Her other hand reached for her mouth again; tears pooled at the corners of her eyelids. "I thought I'd finally run you off for good, lost you forever. I'm so sorry for all I've done to hurt you, so sorry for everything—"

"It's okay, Mom. It's okay," I whispered, leaning forward to lock her in a tight embrace. My knees found the floor next to her wheelchair and my body began to heave with weighty sobs, back shaking as I let them rack my body. "I already know. I forgive you, I do, I do, I do." The burning was gone now; my temples no longer throbbed. A soft, peaceful humming vibration replaced the pain. After what seemed hours, Mom and I pulled back from one another, and shared a box of tissues to wipe at our tears.

"Are you seeing a man?" she asked, catching sight of the ring on my finger.

"It was a sort of elopement," I held out my finger for her. "We didn't invite anyone, so ..."

"I understand. Does he treat you good?"

"He does. You'd love him. In fact—"

"Is he here? In Seattle?"

"Yeah. And he'd love to meet you. But he wanted

me to have some alone time with you first." I slid my cell phone from my pocket, texted Gavin, and within a few minutes, there was a soft knock on the door. Mom worked to blot the last of her tears from her cheeks when Gavin walked in. He reached down to shake her hand.

"It's great to meet you, Ms. Hart. *Er ...* that's not your last name anymore, is it? Uh ... should I call you—?"

"Thank you, thank you," she blinked up at him and stole a glance in my direction. "It's fine. You can call me Karen." She adjusted her shirt collar and smoothed her hair. "Well, this is a lot to take in. You certainly are handsome. You two will make beautiful grandbabies for me someday."

"Mom," I rolled my eyes, lips turning up in a smile. Although children weren't exactly a priority and I doubted frozen souls even had kids, I had to hand it to her. She was right. Any child with Gavin's DNA would be genetically blessed, that was certain.

"Would you both like to stay for an early lunch or something? Gavin, can I fix you some coffee?"

"Thanks, Karen, but we've just eaten. Is that Camille there?" He'd noticed the array of photographs on the mantel over my mother's shoulder, and that launched them into conversation about my childhood. I snuck around the corner into the kitchen and grabbed the notepad by the phone, then cleared some counter space to write. Their chatter floated in from the living room. It was a comforting sound, one I wanted to remember.

Scribbling, I decided to keep it short and sweet. *Live*

life for me, Mom. Forgive yourself. I love you always, Cam.
Pinning the note under a magnet on the refrigerator, I
glanced around the kitchen and returned to the living
room to find Gavin seated on the couch, the laugh lines
around his mouth defined, eyes warm as he listened to
my mother. Clearing my throat from the doorway, the
stinging flared up again, causing me to flinch. My mom's
head snapped toward me and it was back—the anxiety,
evident on her face, and pulsing through my body. She
wondered when she'd see me again, or if she'd ever see
me again at all: wanted to know if I truly forgave her for
all she'd done. The thoughts came to me as quickly and
clearly as they had with the lost little boy.

"Camille, are you okay, love?" Gavin stood, his face
full of concern.

Rubbing my temple with two fingers, I nodded,
focusing on what I needed to say to diffuse my mother's
fear. "Mom, I'm sorry, but we have to get going. But
listen," I crossed the room and kneeled next to her,
glancing up at Gavin. He leaned down and shook Mom's
hand once more, wished her well, and slipped out the
front door.

"Please don't worry about me, and I'll come visit
again as soon as I can … when I have more time. We'll
do dinner at SkyCity. Sound good?" I sent her a faint
smile, urging her to recall the last time we'd eaten at the
Space Needle together.

Tears shimmered in her eyes again and the pain in
my temples subsided as sadness replaced her worry.

"That sounds perfect," she said. "Thank you for coming. And Gavin is … he's just fantastic, honey."

"Yeah, he's a keeper." I winked and kissed her on the cheek with another tight hug, then turned to the front door. She pivoted her chair to watch me exit. Already moving, I said, "Whenever you're scared or worried about me … or about me and you … look to the note on the fridge."

With a deep breath and a curious tilt of her head, she nodded. "I love you, Camille. Have a safe trip home."

"Love you, too. I will."

Gavin waited out front, and his fingers locked into mine. "How's your head?"

"Better now. Wait, how did you know—?"

"You looked as if you were in pain. It was the same pain you felt with the little boy, wasn't it?"

Turning to face him, I took a slow, steady breath, the aftershocks of my mother's anxious emotions still fresh in my veins. "Yes. What does that mean?"

"It means you know who you are as a frozen soul now. You've discovered your reading ability."

Hearing that what I'd dreaded might be happening since my contact with the little boy that day was real, had come to fruition, I screwed my eyes shut, willing the truth away. I'd known I'd eventually discover my reading ability, but I had no idea it would have such a strong pull on me. I hated feeling out of control, the way I did when the burning came. But I had to face it now, and I knew.

I could read fears.

6

OWNERSHIP

The weight of Gavin's words started to sink in. My insides churned with strange excitement, uncertainty—and something else I couldn't identify. Sauntering down my mother's street, hand in hand, he led me between two houses, burying us out of sight behind a gathering of pine trees. The light mist of the midmorning Seattle rain beaded up on my skin.

Gavin said, "Arianna and I believe the little boy was your beacon, the one who initiated your identity."

"And the burning feeling ... that's part of it?"

"Yes. It's strongest right after the change, although you don't notice how it develops until you start spending time around humans. Then it appears in spurts, whenever you make contact with those you can read. Those people will be just as drawn to you as you are to them, so you'll be able to spot them easily. Learning to drain their energy—and to refrain from it—is a matter of meditation. I'll train you, show you how to harness the skill over time."

"But I don't want to drain anyone," I pulled my hand from his and crossed my arms tight across my chest. All I could think of was the way Andrew took advantage of me, how my abusive ex made me his host and fed off my energy the entire time I knew him, even before I knew he was a frozen soul. I wouldn't do that to a human being.

Ever.

I also hadn't forgotten the reason our reading abilities were only compatible with some humans: the human had to possess a strength or natural disposition in whatever emotion from which we drew energy. The fact that I read fears meant I'd be feeding off someone's weakness. I'd be taking advantage of people who were particularly bent toward anxiety, and that was just cruel. Out of all the emotions or personality traits I could have fed from, of course it turned out that I read this one.

Great. Shuddering, I shook my head. "I want to live as you and the resistance do … I won't harm humans the way the other frozen souls do."

"Of course you won't," he reached for my hand again, gently caressing my shoulder. "You have to learn how to control the skill, though, baby. You might need the energy in an emergency … just as I did, the day I drained you to help us escape Samira's castle. Or you'll have to know how to stop yourself from naturally draining someone you don't want to. Pulling that energy becomes very addicting, when you feel the strength it can give you. It requires a lot of restraint." Eyeing the neighborhood's surroundings, he pulled me tighter against him amidst the trees. "But don't worry about that right now. We have enough to deal with when we get home."

Leaning down to place a kiss on my lips, he strengthened his grip around the curve of my back, and we lifted up in flight, leaving the misty rain, fresh pine scents, and my mother behind.

Gavin's plantation home seemed like the proverbial madhouse when we returned that afternoon. Hundreds of frozen souls—too many to count, really—filled every space in the house, gulping down blood, sharpening silver daggers, and practicing combat moves. Vampires all along the stairway, the second floor balcony, and all over the billiard room and library. Vampires. Vampires everywhere. The sight made my head spin.

"So much for being inconspicuous before the showdown," I mumbled to Gavin as he shut the front door behind us. Drawers and cabinets slammed in the kitchen, music blared from upstairs, and wrestling and knife combat sessions littered the main living areas and corridors. Though we didn't know exactly what kind of battle we'd face when we returned to Amaranth tonight—or if physical force could even fight it—we'd worked hard to prepare for anything and everything. Seeing that physical strength, the level of coordination the others had trained for playing out in front of me was comforting. Exhausting, yes, but comforting.

"I mean, really! Is this a briefing for a life-or-death

battle or a damn frat party?" Audrey squeezed through a group of vampires playing cards on the floor and tripped toward us, catching pieces of cheese and three glasses of blood before they slid off the end of her decked-out party tray. "I can't even hear myself think— Hey, you two!" she hollered. Not at us, but at two frozen souls making out up against the wall. "This isn't prom night, people. Practice something more … useful for tonight, will you?"

"Audrey …" I winced when she screeched at more passerby. Apparently they didn't understand her penchant for cleanliness. Her eyes appeared ready to pop from their sockets when she spotted the drinks they'd spilled on her squeaky-clean floor.

"Audrey, I appreciate your concern for the cleanliness of my house and all," Gavin spoke up over the noise, a barely restrained grin on his face, "but you might want to tone it down a notch."

Oh no. I hid my smile with a covering hand, weaving around the two of them, sure I didn't want to be around for this. I had more important things to do, such as find a quiet space in the house to calm down and convince myself that tonight would not be a disaster.

"Tone it *down*?" Audrey's voice squawked. I eyed her over my shoulder as I worked through the crowd to make my way upstairs. She set the tray down and her hands were on her hips. *Oh, shit*, I thought, watching. *She's thrown down the gauntlet.*

Gabe and Arianna were chatting at the top of the

staircase. Gabe met me with an amused smirk. He shot a glance down at the feud, taking a healthy swig of beer. "Gavin is so screwed."

"Yup," Arianna craned her neck to sneak a peek. "He'll be stuck down there for at least twenty more minutes." The three of us shook our heads at the sight of Gavin peering up at us over the crowd, his chocolate brown eyes screaming, "*Help me. For the love of God, help me.*"

Shrugging, we erupted into a fit of laughter, and began filling one another in on the day's events. After relaying the news about my reading ability and the meeting with my mom, I snuck away for a quick smoke break, returning to find the atmosphere had shifted dramatically throughout the house. The music had silenced, the laughter and shouting turned to whispers and intense expressions on everyone I could see. Gavin and Arianna had taken center stage, addressing everyone with equal intensity.

Though I knew it, I listened while Gavin's strident, commanding voice described the plan, which was to set up a distraction when we arrived at the bayou portal, Gavin at the head of the resistance, front and center, to face Gérard, who would surely be waiting at the portal for us. A group of frozen souls was to cause a commotion seconds before the portal opened, to start a fight with Gavin to distract Gérard, while others from the resistance helped cover me so I could enter the portal with Arianna.

Lame, old-fashioned, human trickery at its best.

But it was all we had, our only chance to sneak someone through the portal to get a head start in meeting Samira. And because of Gavin's general over-protectiveness and my freakish link to the Book of the Ancients, I'd been the one appointed to get to Samira as fast as possible and share the message from Vivienne, hopefully convincing Samira to return Dali and Akim to human form at lightning-fast speed. Oh, and then hope the pair of wolves-turned-human even listened to what I had to say.

Right. Things were looking brighter by the second.

Gavin's voice boomed over the room, his take-charge swagger in full-out strut mode, the stance he adopted whenever he resumed his leadership role that made more than a few of the frozen souls throughout the house all starry eyed. The shy, reserved Gavin was charming. Gavin the leader was mesmerizing.

His gaze was locked on mine, scanning the others every few moments to assure them he was confident we'd do what we went to Amaranth to do the first time around: bring down the exile and reclaim freedom from the curse for all.

"I won't lie to you all," he said, shuffling his silver dagger from palm to palm. "As you already know, we weren't expecting Gérard's demands to enter Amaranth with him. And the odds don't look good for us even without that. But with Arianna standing with us and whatever the witches' Book of the Ancients has been leading us toward, I stand to reason that we'll have the opportunity to end this once and for all. Try your damnedest—every single one of you—to make it through that portal, and report to Samira as quickly as possible. But our priority is getting Camille and Arianna through first, no matter what. Right now, Camille is the most valuable to our mission. She's being directed by the Book of the Ancients. And Arianna, being Samira's weak spot, is Camille's safeguard. So it's imperative to get them both to Amaranth first."

Gavin had left out the part that he, too, was pretty crucial to this mission. He was deemed "the beginning of things to come" by the witches, after all. But he seemed to believe leading the others and putting himself on the frontline with them was the focus of his destined duty. And once he had that responsibility in his head, there was no arguing with him.

Raising his glass and sliding his knife into his belt, he nodded to the sea of frozen souls scattered around the house. "To strong will, sweet freedom, and sending this conjure son of a bitch to his grave, where he belongs." He cleared his throat uncomfortably, glancing at Arianna. "No offense."

"None taken," she replied, repeating his battle declaration aloud while raising her glass until every vampire in the house was shouting, chanting, echoing this mantra, causing the room's wooden floors and the walls to shake. The vivacious energy was contagious, the charge in the air palpable and fierce. Slipping the Book of the Ancients into my watertight backpack and adjusting the straps tight over my shoulders, I made my way through the crowd toward Mr. Beginning-of-Things-to-Come and pressed my lips against his, drawing strength from his strength, and hope from the family that surrounded me. If I were destined to be some kind of firestarter in all this mess, it was time I reached way, way down, where the courage cowered beneath the terror, and be ready to light that match.

***

Holding Gavin's hand as he led us all into the bayou, I couldn't help but wonder how many of the faces behind me I'd see again after tonight. The fact that we had no magic on our side this time, and were about to face Gérard again, added to the horrific reality that I might also lose Gavin.

And that took the wind right out of me.

Stopping short, I inhaled deeply, the call to run tingling in my fingertips. But now wasn't the time. The sun was drifting lower toward the earth, the crescent moon imminent.

Gavin stopped with me and gently held up a hand to gesture to everyone behind us to halt. Leaning close, he guided me forward against his chest by the small of my back. "Hey," he whispered. "Don't you dare worry about me."

I lifted my chin to meet his gaze.

"It's all over your face, baby. You don't have to say it. But I need for you to not worry about what happens to me tonight, do you hear me?" Taking my chin between his fingers, he pressed his forehead to mine. "Don't give me that look. If what Clea said is true, and this book is steering us the right way, we have nothing to fear. If she didn't believe it would work, Vivienne wouldn't have made it a priority to create a link to relay all this information to you. What have the witches been saying to us? *It's all written.*"

Unable to deny that he had a point, I nodded, clutching his chest. "You're right. It's just … you heard what Clea said. All of this might be fate, but the outcome can change if we screw up. What if we fail?"

"Then we fail together. But we won't."

"You all might die, trying to get us through the portal," I clutched his shirt tighter between my fingers. "What if you were in my shoes? Do you understand how painful it is for me to even consider the possibility?" Sneaking a glance behind us at Audrey and Gabe, my throat tightened. There they stood, our most precious human friends, with nothing more to protect them than a few measly silver knives and the scant hope in a prophetic book that some voodoo-hoodoo witches told us to follow.

It was all so crazy, and yet here we were. Again.

I felt his fingertips on my chin and he rotated my face to meet his. "I know it's not what you want to hear, Cam, and damn if I hate saying it. But, if me … if that's what it takes to get you to the other side, then that's my role in all this. I've accepted that. Don't you think I feel the same? Not long ago, you were a normal human girl going about your life. And now you're like me, somehow branded to play a part in *my* mess, *my* mission. In the wildest dream I've ever had, I never would have guessed you'd be dragged in this deep. But for some reason beyond my understanding, *it was written*. You're the one with the visions, the one Vivienne imparted the information about the wolves to. So you're the one Samira will listen to, especially with Arianna by your side. This is the way it has to be. Just remember, the moment you step foot on the other side, stick with Ari and get to her mom come hell or high water. Use all the moves I taught you to protect yourself if the guards try to stop you. As soon as Ari's in range, she'll contact Josh to let him know you guys are there."

Tracing the curve of my jaw with his thumb, he seared me with a slow, wet kiss and returned my hand to his with a soft squeeze.

We moved forward again and the resistance followed, twigs, leaves, and damp muck crunching beneath our feet as we approached the familiar oak tree with the magic branch, the one that opened the bayou portal. Coming to a full stop in the swampy clearing, Gavin and I turned around to face everyone, Audrey, Gabe, and Arianna moving to stand next to us.

With a subtle nod to the resistance, Gavin threaded his fingers through my hair, his breath hot on my face as he leaned down to press his lips to mine. "See you on the other side, baby."

"See you," I whispered against his mouth, steeling myself when he broke our connection. I eyed the impending darkness looming above us, the faint trace of the sunset's glow dressing the twilight. Gavin disappeared amongst the mass of frozen souls, positioning himself in its center as they formed a protective bubble around him toward the outer layer of our group, while another handful of vampires joined Audrey and Gabe to barricade Arianna and me against the bayou's bank. I was nestled against the edge, ready to take the leap the instant the water began to churn. More formations of frozen souls lined the other sides of the bayou, some nestled in the surrounding trees, all working together to bury us from sight and to keep us as close to the opening as possible.

An eerie cracking sound echoed in the distance, the wind beginning to build. The temperature dropping, Audrey and Gabe at once zipped up their sweatshirts to warm their human skin. We had no idea from which direction Gérard would come at us, and for all we knew, he could swoop in from overhead and throw us awry. Something about being low and flat to the ground made me feel massively vulnerable, and I gripped my dagger tight in my palm at the thought.

One of the vampires I'd seen practicing combat moves back at the house was stationed next to the magical oak tree, one hand planted firmly on the door-key branch, ready to snap it the moment the crescent moon became fully visible.

The branches and leaves rustling around us, the swamp came to life with movement, the wind quickening by the second, the sunset nearly gone. Low murmurs began to spread throughout the sea of vampires, their stances visibly shifting when a clearing appeared amidst the trees. I kept my head down, peeking desperately through the bodies to catch a glimpse of Gérard. No luck, but though my view was completely blocked, I could make out his chilling voice. It became clearer, and judging by the body language of the frozen souls in front of me, they were already terrified. Knees were crouched, some of their legs shifting with quivering shakes. Others grasped the backs of the ones next to them for support.

"He's not alone," Arianna whispered, gripping my arm so tight I could feel her fingernails draw blood.

"What do you mean, he's not alone?" Glancing up toward the horizon again, I could make out the trees with their dressings of swaying moss, their leaves shaking and bristling against some kind of force. Crouching next to Arianna, I followed her gaze as she worked to peek through the crowd.

"Witches!" she whispered. "Witches everywhere, there must be at least twenty … wait. More than that, oh my God …"

"That doesn't make sense." Frantic, I glanced around. "Their magic doesn't work on us, what good will that do—?"

Gérard's voice was clear, and loud enough to address the entire crowd.

"My dear children, some friends have accompanied me to ensure this whole process runs as quickly and efficiently as possible. I've linked our powers together, you see. So although their magic would have no effect on you by itself, when tuned into mine," a haughty laugh escaped his lips, "well, you get the picture. Now, you can all do this the easy way and allow me to escort you through the portal, or my friends and I can simply take care of that ourselves."

My shaking knees dug into the dirt as I stooped to the ground next to Arianna.

"I'm right here, Gérard." Gavin's voice sounded from the center of the resistance's formation. "But you won't be escorting any of us anywhere."

Every muscle in my body clenched at hearing Gavin's voice, heard it moving, shifting in direction as the vampires cleared a path straight down the middle to make way for him. I was only able to manage one glimpse, but it was enough to send new tremors down my body.

A row of witches lined the perimeter next to Gérard, hands locked to form a wall, and Gavin was making his way through the others straight for them. I shifted my gaze up, zoning in on the crescent moon, and I nudged Arianna.

What happened next transpired so fast, my mind didn't have time to catch up with my body's reflexes.

Arianna signaled the next frozen soul in command to signal the vampire at the magical oak. The branch snapped on cue, and the bayou's watery vortex began swirling behind us, the violet light emanating from its magical depths. A volley of tormented screams erupted from the front lines and rolled its way backward toward us, and bodies of frozen souls soared upward and outward, catapulting in every direction as Gérard's force propelled them from the ground. Some darted and retreated into the trees, their faces full of terror, while others poured into the water behind us and surrendered themselves to the portal's pull.

"Come on, come on, come on!" Arianna cried, pulling me to the edge of the water, ready to fling us straight into the portal opening to follow the others. Complete chaos all around us, my gut dropped when I craned my neck around to get one last peek at Gavin before we plummeted into the water. I had to know if he was among the growing casualties. My heart shuddered at the thought while my eyes searched. No sign of Gabe or Audrey, either. My attention was taken by Gérard. Most of the shield the frozen souls had created around Arianna and me had been broken up, bodies scattered everywhere, creating a path that placed me clear in his view. His gaze locked onto mine.

Before Arianna could jerk my hand forward to launch us into the water, Gérard's force seized me, freezing me in place then flipping me around so I was facing him. The same heavy, thumping pain that had appeared the day he confronted me at Gavin's house radiated in my chest. Ribcage rattling beneath my skin, I reached for my heart, cried out and squeezed my eyes shut from the pain, opening them briefly to catch his stone-cold glare burning a hole in my chest, eyes narrowing when they lowered on my necklace. One hand raised in front of him, he reached out and gripped at the air, his fingers clenching into a ball so forcefully his knuckles whitened.

"Father! No!" Arianna screamed beside me, and the witches, still hand in hand, tightened their link next to Gérard, their sets of beady eyes burning into my skull, chanting so loudly the battle cries of the frozen souls around us were drowned out. Everything moved in half motion then; a slow, wicked smile rolled across Gérard's lips, his force shooting me forward across the muddy ground, sending me straight to him. The toes of my boots skimmed the earth and my body surged forward, jerking to a stop a few inches in front of him. I slumped to the ground with a hard thud and gasped when I peered up to find that the same unseen force he'd used to pull me to him had blasted him backward into the trees.

Not even he could hide his surprise, which turned to outrage when he realized what was happening. The witches continued their chanting, but now their focus was directed at him, their furious expressions zoning in on him as they shifted their linked wall to watch him fly over their heads. I didn't get a chance to see where he'd landed or what the witches were about to do to him next, because a few of them broke away from the link and powered toward me, lifting me and rushing me back in the other direction, straight toward the water, where—oh, thank the sweet, sweet Lord—Gavin, Arianna, Audrey and Gabe all waited.

"What's going on?" I shouted to the witches who guided me. The wind sent my long tendrils into a flurry, whipping at my neck and cheeks.

"We're taking back what's ours," one of them called out. "Hurry, now go!"

Handing me over to my friends, they helped push us all into the bayou's muck-ridden, purple abyss, and Gavin and I latched onto one another as the watery cyclone tugged at our knees and swallowed us. The last thing I saw before my head went under was the row of witches who'd helped us, their bodies simultaneously dropping to the ground in lifeless, ghoulish lumps beneath the moonlit sky.

7

FRIENDS AND ENEMIES

Everything ached, even as the warm water soothed and swirled over my skin, its force pulling us more strongly, relentlessly toward the bayou's muddy floor. My eyes were screwed shut, only sensing the rays of blinding purple light around us as we descended to the bottom, and finally, through the portal hole that would lead us to the other side, to the Amaranth exile.

The bayou's floor swallowed us up and pulled us down through the tunnel, and a head rush accompanied the aching feeling when I dropped from the end of the tunnel and smacked onto the familiar black-and-white-tile floor, Gavin breaking my fall as best as he could. We darted away from the spot, knowing, at any second, more frozen souls would be falling through the portal hole from above and landing on top of us. Drenched and covered in muck and leaves, Gavin swiped dirt from his eyes and pulled me down the long underground hallway toward the door that led up and out, into the beautiful sea of green toward Samira's castle. There were no words, no time for any exchanges, only rapid action to reach our next destination.

Sure enough, those left of the resistance charged the tunnel behind us as each dropped from the portal hole, rushing with us to the door at the end of the passage, Arianna, Gabe, and Audrey thankfully among them. The candlelight flickered, casting an eerie glow through the underground walkway. Our friends coughed to expel the water and dirt from their noses and throats. I wondered how many more times I'd have to cross through that dreaded portal, the one that always seemed to throw my life into full-on crisis mode, bringing with it a multitude of dangers and certainly no guarantees.

That musing halted when Gavin cracked the jagged door wide open, and it welcomed us with a cascade of gloomy sunlight and a dust-ridden cloud of air. Once outside, Gavin and I stepped aside with Arianna, Gabe, and Audrey, while the other frozen souls poured past us and into flight, up and above the vibrant maze toward the castle.

I turned to my friends. "What the hell is going on? Did I just imagine that, or did all of those witches just … *turn* on Gérard? How is that possible?"

"No idea." Arianna grabbed hold of my forearm and pulled me into an embrace. "My God, I thought I was going to lose you there for a second." She squeezed me tight, her breathing as shaky as mine. "All I know is, they saved our asses and bought us some time."

"Not much," Gavin said, sizing up the frozen souls

as they flew in droves over our heads. When their trail seemed to dissipate, he turned and swiftly slammed the portal hole's door shut behind us. Not that it would deter Gérard, but I could tell it made Gavin feel better to shut it.

"You're right," Arianna said, glancing over at Audrey and Gabe, who were leaning against the green labyrinth wall, still catching their human breaths. Gabe nodded and gently helped Audrey straighten up. "Gav, you take Aud. Lover boy," Arianna pointed to Gabe, "you're with me. Cam, you lead the way."

"Right away boss," Gavin quipped, kissing me on the cheek before scooping Audrey up. Arianna and Gabe locked into a tight embrace and I shot from the ground, glancing behind to see them follow my lead. We soared over the maze and emerald-green hills toward the castle, its cathedral's shadow stretching out and covering a patch of bright green before us, where throngs of Samira's monstrous guards awaited us. We landed gracefully, albeit the adrenaline rush, sending grateful nods to the resistance as they parted to let us through. Gavin and Arianna remained at my side, keeping tight rein on Gabe and Audrey.

"Go ahead, baby," Gavin said, encouraging me forward through the sea of monsters. It was the strangest feeling, to be spurred ahead by him, when I knew exactly how concerned he was for my safety. Yet I knew why he was doing this: He believed in me, in this, whatever my role was in this production. He didn't need to say it, and that thought sent my heart reeling. With a warm glance in his direction, I turned toward the wall of guards stationed at the front of the moat, where they begrudgingly rotated their formation to lead us inside. We crept forward, the resistance on our heels, through the bizarre rose conservatory and into the main foyer.

The tall wooden doors opened to reveal Samira seated comfortably at her throne.

This meeting felt instantly different from our prior confrontations. Her relaxed demeanor didn't fool me, though. The moment her eyes landed on mine, my energy-reading radar went on red alert, the burning sensations stinging the sides of my temples like tiny electric shocks. I winced. Gavin caught my elbow at the sign of my pain.

"Cam?" he whispered, moving closer.

"I'm fine, I'm fine." Blinking and returning my focus to the statuesque queen before us, I vaguely wondered how I was able to read her well-disguised anxiety. Hadn't she told Gavin that her magic prevented that ability the last time we were here, when she assumed he'd been trying to read her desires? And the day Gérard drained me, Gavin only mentioned that Gérard was able to drain whomever he wished because of who he was—another reason reading Samira's energy seemed even more unlikely: who was I to be able to read this all-powerful hybrid creator's energy?

That vague wonder transitioned into a desperate curiosity.

The last time we were here, in this very throne room, asking her to join us in our mission to destroy Gérard, I'd had a hunch that Gavin's suggestion to form an alliance was a good one. I'd silently encouraged that idea while he challenged her with it, somehow sensing she was unsettled, and that although she would never admit to it, agreeing to the alliance would help diffuse her fear.

I stalled in my tracks, my friends pausing behind me as I planted myself in front of the throne steps. Gavin and Arianna were speaking to me, but their voices were muffled as the memories bombarded me: of the innate empathy I'd harbored for Samira, even before I'd become a frozen soul. When Vivienne and Gavin had shared her history with me, I'd considered the idea that we should somehow try to see things from her point of view, sympathize in some way. It came so naturally, to feel compassion for her. And yet I stuffed that feeling down, forced myself to extinguish it because I knew no matter how natural it felt, it was downright crazy.

Samira stood, carefully clasping her hands together in front of her gown. "Arianna, I'm so glad to see you again—"

"We have news," Arianna cut her off. "And not much time. My father will be here any second. Hurry, Camille. Tell her."

Before I could open my mouth, I buckled over from the pain in my forehead; Samira's fear was flying off the charts. "Samira," I spit out, allowing Arianna and Gavin to hold me up. "Stop, stop!"

"Leave her alone!" Gavin shouted at Samira, latching onto me.

"What are you doing to her, Mother?" Arianna cried.

"I am not doing anything, my child." Samira's eyes flared, bouncing between the three of us in confusion.

I forced my gaze up to meet her, gritting my teeth. This was unlike the little boy—my beacon—unlike my mother, and the earlier fiery pains. This was intense, too intense. "I know it's hard, but I need you to calm down. I can read your fear, can feel it."

"You what?" Arianna and Gavin said in unison, their heads snapping in my direction.

"Samira," I squeezed my eyes tighter, "I know you're afraid of Gérard, but I need you to relax so I can think clearly."

"Camille?" Gavin put his mouth to my ear. "What's going on—?"

"You heard her, Mother!" Arianna shouted. "Relax, because we don't have much time. You need to focus."

Slowly, the pain unraveled in delicate, concentrated layers. Straightening up and keeping my gaze on Samira, I could tell she was working exceedingly hard to rein in her anxiety. Nothing but pure shock registered on her face at the realization that I could, in fact, read her energy. A glance at Gavin and each of my friends told me they felt the same way.

I hurried to take advantage of the lull. "Vivienne couldn't help us. Gérard killed her. We found her dead when we got back to earth. But she sent me a message through a link. You need to turn Dali and Akim human again, immediately." Shifting to pull the Book of the Ancients from my watertight bag, I held it in front of her with pleading eyes. "The wolves are the key to defeating your husband, and I need to speak to them, to find out what they know. The Book of the Ancients has been revealing these things to me ... and this is our only chance. You have to believe me."

Samira scanned the faces of the resistance before parting her lips to speak, her eyes narrowing into threatening slits. "That is utterly absurd. I will do no such thing. How are you able to ... read my emotion? Are you working with the original conjurers again? Are you working against me again? What have you done?"

"Mother," Arianna spat, "we don't know why Camille can read you. We don't have time to mull this over, so cut the bullshit!"

Realizing Samira was one second away from lashing out, I spoke calmly. "When I read you ... the pain is intense. I'm not sure what it means, but look," I flipped open the Book of the Ancients and cautiously approached her throne, showing her the last illustrated page, where the map and the rowboat were drawn to lead Gavin and me to Clea. "The witches are helping us, their book is leading us ... to something." I gestured to the hordes of vampires behind me. "The only way we were even able to cross through the portal and get here is because of what the witches did. I don't know how they did it, but they turned against Gérard, protected us so we could pass through. Said something about taking back what was theirs."

"Yes, Mother," Arianna said. "They showed up with Father at the bayou, they ambushed us, but something happened and they attacked him."

No one moved. The fireplace's crackling bounced off the stone walls into desolate echoes, fueling the escalating tension in the room.

"If this is in fact correct," Samira finally said, "that Dali and Akim are the key to defeating my husband, then he has designed the perfect failsafe."

"Come again?" Gavin asked.

"It is the perfect failsafe because he knows I shall never restore the wolves' humanity." Her chin lifted and her shoulders set, as if to make it clear this conversation was over.

I sure as hell wasn't giving up that easily.

"Your Majesty, this is no time for stubbornness or harboring grudges. When Gavin suggested an alliance to you, something in you told you it was the right thing to do." I shifted my gaze to Arianna, and Samira noticed; she glanced at her daughter before training her eyes back on mine. "You want to destroy him," I said when our gazes met again. "You want freedom just as much as we do, and I know you want to apologize to Arianna for all you've done, and this is the closest shot you're ever going to get." I winced when the stinging pain attacked my temples for a moment, thankful when it ebbed, shifting to a low, hot simmer.

Samira's eyes were shut, her lips bunched tight as she focused to control her fear. As painful as it was to feel the effects of her fluctuating emotion, I was grateful for the confirmation it gave: my assumptions were correct. She was afraid I might be right.

Her gaze curious at the Book of the Ancients I held before her, she moved down the throne steps for a closer look. Raising her eyes to scan the resistance again, she shook her head. "Absolutely not. I do want a chance to earn your forgiveness, my daughter," she looked to Arianna, "more than you'll ever know. However, this is out of the question. I refuse to entertain this foolish idea!"

I turned to Gavin, knowing we didn't have one more second to lose. "How about you go find Josh and check on the Amaranthians? Send the resistance to man the portal entry for Gérard's arrival. It can buy us a few minutes." Twisting around to include Arianna, I channeled every ounce of determination I could muster into my expression. "I need to speak to your mother alone."

"Absolutely not," Gavin jolted forward, body rigid as a rail. "Camille, this is not happening, do you hear me?"

"Gav," I lowered my voice, leaning into him, keeping a viselike grip on the Book of the Ancients. "If you're going to trust me, you have to trust me all the way, do you understand?" I had to get her alone. It was the only way I could try to convince her to do this. She wouldn't let some puny frozen soul order her around in front of such an audience and risk further hurting her pride.

"She's right, Gav," Arianna said, eyes shifting to her mother's throne. "Let her go."

His jaw clenched, his eyes giving away his mind's internal struggle. Swallowing hard, he leaned in and grasped the sides of my face. "I don't like that you can read her … *feel* her so strongly. Whatever you have to say to her, you can say it in front of me."

"No. Leave. *Now*."

"Perhaps you should listen to your wife." Samira's voice carried down the granite stairway, causing Gavin to flinch. His anger was palpable, rolling off him in stifling waves. He turned to pin her with eyes like daggers, and a smug smile painted her face in return.

"Gav, come on." Arianna tugged his shirtsleeve, glancing at Gabe and Audrey and the slew of vampires behind us, waiting for direction.

Gavin pried his hands from my face. "I want to see my mother," he demanded, finally facing Samira.

"She is in the main village, staying with your friend … Josh, I believe. Victor will escort you, and my guards will accompany the rest of you to the portal door." Samira raised her voice, lifting her chin to address the army behind us. "I do believe Camille and I have business to attend to." On cue, Victor appeared from the rear doors, politely extending his long, bony hands to encourage Gavin to follow him.

Gavin shut his eyes in defeat, reopening them to burn me with his gaze. "I can't believe I'm agreeing to this."

"Believe it, because it's happening. Now *go*."

Drawing a sharp breath, he nodded once and stalked toward Victor, while Arianna, Gabe, Audrey, and the frozen souls all followed the guards out the front doors, the sounds of their shuffling footsteps bringing life to the room. I suddenly felt I could breathe again.

The last few guards filtered out behind the resistance, and Samira and I deadpanned one another, locking gazes at lightning-fast speed. I spoke first. "Return Dali and Akim to their human form."

"Tell me everything you know."

"I've already told you, we don't have time for that. I've heard the story, Samira. When Gérard betrayed you, you went into a rage and turned them. You have to let that grudge go."

"A grudge." She let out a dry laugh, began to float down the steps toward me. "You were a resilient mortal, and clearly, are even more resilient as a frozen soul. Which is why I am surprised that a being as strong, as clever as you, has failed to realize there is always more to a story than century-old gossip."

"It doesn't matter! Don't you understand? Look, I understand you're worried they'll … retaliate somehow. They have to be pretty angry with you after what you've done to them, but if you'll just let me talk to them—"

"Clearly, my pet, *you* are the one who does not understand. Dali and Akim represent much more to me than a simple grudge. Yes, I wanted my husband to pay for what he had done, so I chose to punish his closest friends. Only … it backfired. To return them to their human form is not only to admit failure, but to relive every shred of dignity I lost that day."

When she reached me at the bottom of the stairway, we came head to head, her arctic eyes cutting mine like glass. The stinging pricked at my temples, but I could feel its low hum begin to vibrate as Samira fought to manage her anxiety at the discussion of her husband. Whatever she was revealing to me terrified her, made her feel vulnerable, at her precise weakest.

Without thinking, I stretched out my free hand and gripped her wrist to console her, encourage her to continue.

Her eyes widened in disbelief, and then something happened that nearly floored me. The tight creases around her eyes softened and her rigid lips fell at their corners, tears forming in her ducts.

I said, "I know he betrayed you, but Arianna is *alive*, Samira. She's here, right now. And all she wants is for you to make this right. He might have held you captive here, forced you to overlook his kingdom, but you don't have to be a slave to him anymore."

"I will always be a slave to him." Her shoulders sagged, and then the tears came. She gripped my hand, allowed me to latch on harder to her wrist. "Can you not see? As a woman? As a wife? As a former mortal yourself?"

I couldn't see. My own tears blinded me now, my frame caving under the weight of her overwhelming anxiety; it was beyond nerve-wracking for her to reveal this level of vulnerability. Despite the tears, I couldn't pry my gaze from the broken woman before me, this exotic, exquisite queen who had nothing left to hang onto other than fury and spite. It must be an exhausting burden to carry, even for our kind.

"No, I can't imagine that level of betrayal. I'm so sorry for your loss, I truly, truly am. Which is why I want—no, I *need* you to fight, to face those demons. If you do, there might be a chance for us *all* to be free from this."

"My pet, even if I am free from this realm, my will to carry on is depleted. Arianna will never, ever forgive me for the monster I've become. Do you not see the hatred in her eyes when she looks at me? Without her, I have nothing. I've had nothing since she left with the uprising. All that will remain are the memories I have of this wretched place and the day Gérard abandoned me for *her*."

I wiped at my tears, watching her turn to resume her seat on the throne while my mind clicked. "What? He didn't abandon you for Arianna. Wait, what does this have to do with Dali and Akim?"

"They were the fools to relay the message to me. Nothing is worth the pain I will surely endure if I bring them back."

"Message?"

"Of the affair. The one your husband has yet to reveal to you, I presume."

Now it was my turn to approach her. I drifted carefully, step by step, up the stairs to stand at her feet.

"His ex-lover," she said, her voice grave. "The worthless fool you have to thank for the loss of your humanity."

My arms dropped limp to my sides, the Book of the Ancients leaving my grip for the first time since we'd arrived in Amaranth, plunking straight to the granite floor with a thud.

"Your husband … had an affair … with *Scarlet?*"

She nodded, tapping her red nails as she did, her sadness slipping away into some far-off void, where it was swiftly replaced with that emotionless, cold expression I'd grown so used to. "She seduced your husband and enticed him into a relationship, only to use him for his connection with mine. Knowing his father, Sean, and Gérard were friends at the time, she convinced Gavin to have Sean introduce her to Gérard, and then she did what she does best: reach out and take whatever she wants."

Her words crushed me, forcing the images into clear view, images I didn't want to imagine: Scarlet seducing Gavin, Gavin being deceived and discarded after she obtained her goal, and then … oh, God. The mere thought that Gavin and the sinister conjure king who'd just touched me had shared the same woman brought bile to my throat.

The revelation cut to the bone, and Gavin's betrayal cut deeper. What I couldn't accept was that Gavin hadn't told me this. No one had. And here I was, finding it out from the vampire queen herself. Even more inconceivable was the fact that he had greeted Scarlet as a long-lost friend, lied to Vivienne and me about Scarlet's knowledge of Arianna, and had allowed her with open arms into the resistance, putting our entire mission at stake. A million questions begged for answers, but I couldn't think about them now.

In that instant, I knew what I'd felt in the beginning was correct, and the epiphany was beyond enlightening: Samira *was* a victim in all this. She never asked for any of it.

Clarity struck hard and swift, and I reached out to take her hand again. "All the more reason to bring the bastard down."

She opened her mouth to speak, but stopped when the Book of the Ancients lit up at our feet, its cover slamming open and pages flapping frantically before us. Our gazes shot downward; the blank page next to the rowboat map demanded our attention as it filled up with bursts of golden sketches. Samira's eyes flew wide, and the images took shape to reveal an illustration of us, grasping hands as if we were reaching out desperately for one another.

I let go of Samira's hand and took a step back, gasping at the illustration's final touch.

A stream of fire burned between the image of our fingertips, extending from my hand to hers, a fiery torch passing its light. My eyes rolled upward to meet Samira's, and Clea's words burned embers in the pit of my stomach: *Your firestarter is by your side.*

8

DUST TO DUST

The book's glow faded, the cover slammed shut, and I scooped it up as if I were capturing a rabid animal that needed to be detained.

Samira paused, then swiveled around to peer at the fireplace. A stretch of unease settled between us, and I contemplated running. I knew it would be the world's stupidest thing to do at a time like this, and it surely wouldn't solve the enigma before us, but God, did I want to run out of the room and never look back. The Book of the Ancients revealed something I absolutely did not want—Samira was tied to me in some way. Judging from her reaction, she wasn't thrilled about it, either. Yet, just like the unwanted empathy I felt for her, it compelled me, and this time, I knew I had to follow its direction.

Samira cleared her throat and I jumped, the sound startling me from my mind's tailspin. Her expression was determined now, driven and vivacious. "Dali, Akim, come," she said, calling to the wolves, who until now had been hidden in the shadows behind the throne altar.

They slunk forward and seated themselves at her feet. "I am under the impression that this will end very badly for me, my pet." She turned to me. "So to be clear, I want you to relay a message to my daughter when this is all over."

I clutched my chest and stepped closer. "What makes you think *I'll* be around to relay the message?"

She lowered her gaze as if thinking, but disregarded my question. "When I found Arianna had left during the uprising, I imagined her growing old back on earth, having children and grandchildren. Although she would go on to live a normal, mortal life, she would remain immortal in my mind: an eternal earth angel, just what I wanted for her since I first held her in my arms." She lifted the linen cover from the altar to reveal her conjure materials, reached for a bottle of dark green potion. "However, I knew my daughter, knew her spirit. When the truth was revealed to me that you all had planned to use knowledge of her location against me, I admit the news shocked me. Although, I was not shocked by the fact that she was alive after all these years. It did not surprise me that she had once again changed from human to vampire, you see. She always constantly teetered between those two identities, even as a child. Her fascination with each world was truly amusing to witness. What surprised me was that I might have the chance to see her again … even if only for a brief moment."

Unfolding her arms and determinedly pinning them

to her sides, she inhaled deeply. "I cannot take back what I have done as queen of this exile. I cannot undo the image she has of her mother, and will always have. When she appeared during your last visit, when I saw her with my own eyes, I was in awe of the strange grace bestowed upon me, to be able to see her again, as beautiful and as fierce as ever. I knew then that the gift given to me in that moment would be enough to sustain me for the duration of my eternity in this wretched kingdom. She will always be my greatest gift, whether she wants to be or not."

"I understand," I said, hearing Dali and Akim's tired whimpers echo throughout the room, mimicking my own waning patience. I wondered if they were responding to her words, if they heard and understood everything that had happened since they'd been turned to wolves.

With a solemn nod, she clasped her hands together and looked to Dali and Akim. They stared back at her from sleepy eyes, their heads rested on their front paws. "Good. Now that is settled ... I believe it is time to test Vivienne's theory." Wrapping a potion in a red velvet sash as she drifted down the stairs, she gestured with a jerk of her chin for me to follow. "Come quickly," she said, motioning for the wolves to join us.

We hurried out of the throne room and entered a long, winding stairwell that led us to a cell similar to the one that held Gavin the first time I'd found him here in the castle, starved and a prisoner. Samira directed the wolves to the far wall, and ordered the cell's guards to secure the animals' feet with chained restraints.

"Will that be enough to hold them back?" I eyed the cuffs. They were Gérard's old conjure mates, after all. Who knew what kind of wrath they'd stored up for Samira after all these years?

"You mustn't worry," she replied. "They will be mere mortals. When I turned them, they were stripped of their power."

The guards exited and the cell door slammed shut, and I shuffled backward until my back hit the door. Samira's hands began to sway their mystic dance, her head rolling softly to one side while quiet chants flowed from her lips. Taking a drink from her potion, she chucked the glass bottle to the ground, where it burst to flame against the stone floor, then vanished. Her chants grew louder and her head rolled back farther, the whites of her eyes appearing through the slits of her eyelids. A gust of wind rippled through the cell, blowing our hair around our faces, the whole room feeling as if it were floating, projecting to a far-off realm, a castle on a cloud.

Dali and Akim began to howl wildly, and that seemed to agitate the wind, sending it spiraling in frantic, random bursts until Samira wrenched her arms in the air to cease it. I closed my eyes tight, bracing myself for whatever would happen next, but opened them to find the wolves had disappeared, leaving two naked men in their places, curled up against the wall in the same shackles. Samira snapped her fingers, and they were instantly covered with brown drawstring linen pants around their waists and loose white t-shirts with single breast pockets. Their feet remained bare, but their eyes ... their eyes were full of shock, and then fury so great, I was sure it could move mountains.

"You—" one of the men choked, grasping his neck as he spoke. The other man was so surprised by the sound of the other's voice, he jumped back and smacked his head on the wall, wincing from the impact. Every slight movement startled them, and the one who'd tried to speak suddenly became fascinated with his fingers.

"Dali, Akim," Samira acknowledged them, staring at them down her nose as if they were lab rats with some sort of infectious disease.

"You, you," the man tried again to speak. His eyes widened and he found his strength to stand, feeling along the wall to maintain his balance.

"Yes, yes," she said. "I know, I know. I'm terribly sorry for my ... indiscretion. I am certain you and Akim would love nothing more than a healthy dose of revenge, however we do not have time for that nonsense, and I need you to focus on what we have to say."

"You call *that* an apology?" I whispered under my breath, in utter disbelief at her flippant greeting.

"When did I ever say anything about an apology?" She pivoted on her hip to glare at me. "My husband is just as much to blame for their fate." She returned her attention to the helpless men before her to pierce them with the same glare. "He had ample opportunity to help them, and yet he chose to walk away and leave them as animals. Is that not correct, gentlemen?"

The man who'd been identified as Dali spoke again, his face full of disbelief at her words, which I think overshadowed his fury now. Moving forward to look Samira in the eye, he ran a hand through his hair and yelped when the chains cut at his feet with the movement. "Is this really necessary?" he shouted, gesturing to the shackles and throwing his hands in the air. "I have nothing! Nothing!"

Samira planted a hand on her hip, her red nails lightly tapping her corset. "I suppose you have a point." Snapping her fingers once more, the restraints disappeared, and Akim stood to join Dali, both of them rubbing their wrists and ankles.

"What … year is it?" Akim asked, voice raspy. He too, must have been overwhelmed by disbelief, because instead of anger, his expression was one of shock mixed with curiosity at the answer. He peered over Samira's shoulder at me, and I stared back at him, transfixed by his crystal blue eyes, which were set under dark lashes against rich, mocha skin. He was utterly breathtaking, and his friend was just as beautiful, with the same dark complexion and startling bright eyes. The men must've been in their mid-thirties when they were turned to vampires or wolves way back—I didn't know when— because they clearly hadn't aged and appeared to be around the same age as Gérard.

"It doesn't matter," Dali huffed, shaking his head. "I

don't even want to know."

"Like hell, it matters!" Akim shouted. "I want to know! How long have you kept us, you despicable wench?"

Samira's wrist swirled before her and he flew backward into the wall. She took a step forward to meet him at eye level. "Tread very carefully when choosing that term to describe me. We all know who the true wench is in this scenario."

He stared back at her and a million different emotions flashed in his eyes, as if he were remembering a multitude of memories at once.

"Let him go, Samira." Dali let out an exhausted sigh and plopped down to the ground, crossing his arms over his knees. "What is it you want from us?"

She paused for a beat before dropping her wrist, letting Akim's feet touch the ground again. He gripped his throat and clenched his jaw, eyes still burning into hers.

"Go on, Camille," she said. "Relay your message."

My eyes fluttering between her and the two men, I cautiously stepped forward. "Well, um ..."

"Oh for heaven sakes," Akim grunted, sitting down next to Dali. "What now? Please, enlighten me." He stared up at me, impatience on his face, and the words caught in my throat.

At last I managed, "You ... you two were Vivienne's ancestors ... is that correct?"

"Vivienne ... as in original conjurer Vivienne? Yes, so?"

"So, she passed away not long ago and before she did, she sent me a message. That I needed to convince Samira to turn you human again."

Dali's face fell at the mention of Vivienne's death, and he rubbed at his eyes with the heels of his hands. "Well isn't that bloody lovely. She was a good woman. And what would the point of that message be, exactly?"

I turned and pulled the Book of the Ancients from my bag. Dali and Akim flew forward and in an instant, were in my face. My nostrils flared at their closeness, and I realized I was starving. The proximity of their warm blood was too much; I needed to get to the others and feed soon.

"Who are you and what are you doing with that?" Akim reached out to take the book but I pulled back.

"Um, yeah ... no offense or anything, but this thing is pretty important right now. I think I'll hang on to it, if you don't mind."

"Well no kidding it's important, love! What in the bloody hell is going on here?"

"This book is giving me direction. I'm no one, just ..." *The firestarter.* I gulped, not ready to relay whatever that meant just yet. "Just a frozen soul who somehow got tied up in this crazy prophetic mess of yours. You're the ones who are supposed to tell me what to do next. That's what Vivienne and Clea, her link—told me, anyway."

"Clea?" Akim's eyes bugged out of his head. "That crazy old bat is still alive, yeah?"

Dali chuckled, coughing as he did. "I remember that

woman. One of the other original witchy loons from back in the day. She must be thousands of years old by now. Her magic is impressive however."

I bit my lip, waiting for him to focus. "Yeah, anyway, she said you two were the key to destroying Gérard, and that you would know what to do."

Dali and Akim exchanged glances. "Destroy him, ay?" Akim muttered, turned and started to pace the cell. "Well the bloody bastard did leave us to rot after his darling of a wife here turned us into those mangy mutts."

Samira shifted an eyebrow, her blood-red nails tapping her clenched waist.

"He was our dearest mate." Dali punctuated this with a sarcastic laugh. "I remember those minutes, right after we were turned to wolves, how he looked at us for a moment. Just stared, like he'd discovered some delightful surprise or something. Then he turns and strolls out of the room. Just like that. The no-good wanker. So we have answers for you, ay?"

I glanced at Samira and cleared my throat. "I hope so. There's been a resistance movement building for years now, made up of all the frozen souls who want the vampire curse destroyed. And to do that, we need to defeat Gérard. The witches turned against him at the portal entry, to buy us some time to get here and speak to you, but I don't know how long we have before he shows up to retaliate. We already pissed him off before that, so I think we're pretty screwed either way."

Dali's eyes narrowed and he began biting his lip.

"The witches turned against him … that's not possible. Unless—"

"They were tapped into his magic somehow," Akim finished for him.

I shrugged. "Maybe, I don't know. They were all joined together when we—my friends and I—arrived at the bayou. Linked hands and everything. They ambushed us."

Both Dali and Akim exhaled, and it looked to me as if their brains hurt from the overload of information they were trying to process. It couldn't be easy trying to understand and keep up with everything Samira and I were throwing their way like this.

I myself exhaled. "Look. A lot has happened since you've been gone. I know you don't know me, and you have thousands of questions, and I'm really sorry for … what's happened to you. But all I know is, this book, and Vivienne and Clea's messages, are guiding us to destroy Gérard. And if we can do that, then the vampire curse is lifted."

Dali turned to grip the cell window's bars. "Well," he snuck a glance at his friend, "we do know how to kill him, if that's what you want to know. Only I don't under-stand one thing."

"One thing?" Samira and I had asked as one.

He shifted his gaze between Samira and me, searching our faces for something. "He knows we know how to destroy him. We practiced magic with him from the very beginning, know his oldest secrets. I doubt he'd just let you and your friends—whoever they are—wander over here and have a chat with us. We must be missing something." His eyes roamed our faces again, squinting in thought.

"But he didn't just let us by," I said. "He and the witches ambushed us at the bayou in hopes of capturing us and taking us into exile ... or doing away with us. And he didn't want me to come here, to you. He spoke to me, through his thoughts, when I first met him. Said something about being careful what I do to save my friends. I think he was referring to this." I gestured between the four of us.

"That might be the case," Dali said, "but leaving something like that to chance is far too risky for him. It doesn't add up."

Samira shook her head, exasperated. "Well there is no use debating this, you fools. We are here now, and he is not, so tell us what you know before it is too late!"

I spoke up, ready to voice my agreement, but sounds of bickering echoed through the hall, followed by a guard peering in through the cell door. "Your Majesty, a Gavin and Josh to see you?"

"*Ttsssk.* " She spun toward the door and fanned out her gown. "Let them in at once."

The door creaked open, and in stepped Gavin and thank God, Josh at his side, both of them looking as if they'd seen a ghost the instant their eyes fell upon Dali and Akim. Then Gavin looked at me and his face changed—becoming a dead giveaway that he knew I'd

found out about Scarlet's history with him and Gérard—
and I returned his expression with one full of ice.

I'd deal with that later.

"Camille, I needed to make sure you were okay," he
said, cutting Samira a glance. "You haven't eaten," he
lowered his voice. "I've sent my mother with Arianna
and the others."

Samira hissed and planted herself firmly in front
of Dali and Akim. "We were just about to retrieve the
information we needed, so if you two fools don't mind
… go on. What must we do?"

"We should … do this somewhere else," Dali said,
crossing his arms.

"Yes, take us to the haven," Akim said, "it's safer
there—"

Samira's magic blew them clear across the cell and
pinned them to the wall, her arms held high, straining
with her force to hold them in place. "I believe we have
wasted enough time filling you idiots in already! Now
tell us what we must do, or I will do this the hard way!"

"Samira …" I cleared my throat, feeling my temples
begin to throb. "Maybe they're right. Maybe we should
listen to them."

She swung around to face me, then pointed her glare
at Gavin. "Any word on his whereabouts? How much
time do we have?"

"I'm not sure," he said. "We haven't heard a word
from the frontlines at the portal entry since we arrived.
It's been quiet. Too quiet."

"What is this 'haven' location you speak of?" she said.

Dali and Akim looked to me, Gavin and Josh, and I wondered who should break the news of the Amaranthians' hideout.

I went first. "Uh ... it's a sort of ... hideout. For the Amaranthians."

"Gérard doesn't know about it," Dali helped me out. "It was put there long ago for emergencies."

This news surprised even me. Why would Gérard's closest conjure mate even know about the haven, let alone keep it a secret from his friend?

Samira studied our faces, and I could tell she wanted to know more, wanted to know how the location could've remained such a secret when right under her nose for so long. "Very well," she said, seething, pinching the bridge of her nose. This calmed her anxiety a hair and I was relieved from the pain's pressure. "To the haven at once."

Storming past Gavin, Josh and me, she allowed her magic to fling the cell door open and charged through it. The rest of us raced out after her, and with the news that the frontlines had been eerily quiet since our arrival, I couldn't help but ponder Dali's earlier statement: we must be missing something.

9

DÉJÀ VU

"Will you at least look at me?" Gavin's hushed voice was at my ear, but I wasn't interested. We were making our way through Amaranth's gates and down the steep incline into the main village's valley. I was much more concerned with seeing the state of Amaranth since we were last here, since the flood and destruction wiped it out, and in focusing on our mission with Dali and Akim.

"No, and I'm not speaking to you about this now. The damage is done."

"I'm sorry I didn't tell you … tell you all the details. You should have heard it from me."

"Oh, really? You think?" I shot him a cold glare, working to keep pace with the others in front of us. Dali and Akim led the way, Samira on their heels, and Josh, Gavin and me behind them. Josh's sweet puppy-dog face had lost its usual luster; the dark circles under his eyes and worn-out expression weighed heavy on him. I wondered when he'd last fed. He seemed to easily tune out of our conversation, hands limp in his pockets as he shuffled behind Samira. Being here to help pick up the pieces after we left him to watch over the Amaranthians couldn't have been easy.

"You never asked, so I didn't volunteer the information," Gavin said. "You knew Scarlet and I had a history … but I should've told you about her affair with Gérard and that she knew about Arianna."

Okay, I changed my mind. We were going to have it out right now, because he owed me so much more of an apology, and explanation, than that.

I stopped walking and spun to look at him. "I don't care about the affair, Gavin. What I *care* about is the fact that your history extended a bit longer than you led me to believe. If she was using you to get to your dad and Gérard, that means you were with her long before you were a 'new, lonely, reckless vampire,' as you put it. What I *care* about is that you lied from the beginning—to me and Vivienne—about Scarlet's knowledge of who Arianna was. You swore no one else knew about her identity, and made a huge deal over keeping it secret. And what I *care* about is that you deliberately lied the last time we were here, when you told me you had no idea how Scarlet found out Arianna was Samira's daughter. You knew how all along! All that crap you spewed about someone else *informing* her? You've spun nothing but a web of lies! Do you need any more of an explanation for why I can barely stand to look at you?"

"You're right," he said, and stuffed his hands in his pockets. "For one, I feel like a complete idiot for letting her use me the way she did back then. And secondly, Arianna doesn't know … about Scarlet and her dad. She knows her dad abandoned her mother, but she doesn't know the details. I don't talk about it, okay? And I would appreciate it if you'd leave out that piece of information. Ari's been through enough. She never liked Scarlet much in the first place, and she'd have a conniption fit if she knew what went down between Scarlet and her dad. I shouldn't have lied. It was a horrible thing to do. But I had good intentions."

I turned and resumed my walk, the others ahead of us now, nearly at the village's entrance. "I feel like I don't even know you. If you can keep something like that from me, and bring *her* here with us … how can I ever trust you again? You jeopardized our safety while you played hero."

"The affair was eons ago, Camille. Gérard tossed Scarlet aside when he was done having fun with her, and that was the end of it. It made sense all these years later for her to show up, wanting to be a part of the resistance. I genuinely believed she wanted revenge on Gérard just as much as the rest of us did. And when she pulled that stunt the last time we were here, threatening to expose our plan to Samira, I had to lie to you, *had* to give in to her demands! Not only for the sake of our mission, but for Arianna's sake. Scarlet had me right where she wanted me, and it was too late to backpedal. It was a poor lapse in judgment, and if I could take it all back, I would."

All the tension from the day's events took over and I couldn't hold back.

"A poor lapse in judgment?" I shrieked and stopped walking. "More like a massive, unbelievably stupendous fuckup!" My palm met his cheek with a loud slap, and everyone turned around to stare, jaws dropped. "Because you let that deceitful, no-good bitch into our mission, I am a frozen soul! Cecile is dead, along with countless Amaranthians, and she sold us out to Gérard, too: which means she's responsible for Vivienne's death as well! Do you get that?"

He grabbed my elbow, forcing me to meet his fiery eyes, which was hard because the mere sight of him left me fuming. "What was I supposed to tell Arianna, Camille?" he implored. "When Scarlet caught word of the resistance and wanted to join us, I couldn't tell her no. She threatened to tell Arianna all the gory details about the affair. I did what I thought was best at the time, and in retrospect, yes, it was a monumental fuckup and I'll never live it down, okay? Look, I went back to Scarlet … after I became a frozen soul. I'm telling you now, so you don't hear it from anyone else. I *was* lonely, and I *was* reckless, and she was … familiar. But I promise you, on my mother's life, that's the extent of our history and I haven't withheld anything else from you." He let go of my elbow. "I understand you feel betrayed, but aren't you kind of calling the kettle black?"

"Excuse me?" My eyes narrowed, voice dripping with fury.

"You heard me. What happened between you and Gérard back at the house, Camille? And what the hell is going on with you and Samira, huh? Don't pretend you don't know what I'm talking about. Or could it be that whatever it is, you're not telling me because you're trying to protect me?" He stepped closer, his jaw rigid and eyes stone. "Trying to protect *us?*"

Josh cleared his throat and stepped in, parting us before more damage was done. "Kids, can we skip the *Jerry Springer* episode? It's not the time." Shifting his gaze to mine, Josh pleaded with his eyes, and I could tell the affair was no surprise to him. "Gavin's telling you the truth, Cam. His motive was protecting Ari. Besides, don't forget, it's that damn book that's led us to where we are right now. This is bigger than us. Bigger than the petty parts we've played."

Before I could respond, the three of us were jerked, midair, toward Samira, her hand balled in a tight fist as she directed us with her magic, until we were crumpled up in pain at her feet. I peered up from the ground to find Dali and Akim staring down at us, along with a few glimpses of nearby villagers who were also catching the show.

"Good thinking, Samira," Dali muttered. "Enough of the bloody soap opera. Let's get on, shall we?" He and Akim turned and stalked into the village, and Samira gave us another warning with a jolt of her magic, lifting us from the ground and then slamming us back down, her eyes daggers. She flung her gown's train behind her and forged ahead after them.

Gavin, Josh and I pulled ourselves up and didn't speak another word, wading forward into the village. The sight left my insides aching. Wheelbarrows, mounds of hay, broken furniture and all kinds of debris littered the cobblestone streets. The building structures had taken quite a beating; it was a ghost town all around us. The Amaranthians lined the streets and doorways, faces long and drawn, their stares burning holes into our heads as we passed through. Only the crunches and cracking of our steps could be heard, along with echoes of sobs pouring from a nearby alley. These people had lost everything in an instant. So many of the vampire-turned-human friends and family members they'd resided with were gone, taken from them by the demolishing, prophetic floodwaters.

We remained silent as we made our way toward the windmill and rounded Preservation Hill to the haven, its door buried alongside the hill, camouflaged in green and brown. Dali and Akim unlocked the heavy latch and held the door open, allowing us to descend the stairway that led into the underground cave, Samira leading the way into the darkness. She descended farther and stopped halfway, turning back to glance up at Gavin, Josh and me, and then past us to Dali and Akim, who were still at the top of the stairs. The gloomy sunlight illuminated the edges of their figures, their faces expressionless.

"Well," Samira said, straightening her posture, "you have dragged us to this ridiculous hole in the ground.

Do make haste." She waved impatiently, urging them to follow.

Dali relaxed his shoulders, a faint smile springing up on his lips. "You're right, Samira, we are short on time." He exchanged looks with Akim, who was now sporting a small smile of his own. "We have been tied up for a while and don't want to waste another second. So we'll be running along now, thanks. You're no longer needed."

Confusion filled Samira's face and I felt my own face blanch as I looked to Gavin and Josh for an explanation.

They didn't have one.

"Friends?" Akim pointed to us, amused by our puzzled expressions. "Come on mates, follow us."

"What is the meaning of this?" Samira hissed, taking a few steps forward, at once swirling her hands in the air to work her magic on Dali and Akim. Shock registered on her face and her eyes darted down to her hands—her magic wasn't coming to her aid. "I demand an explanation!" She tried to direct her force toward Dali and Akim again to no avail, and then, turning to Gavin, Josh and me, she began to recite a spell of some sort. Her face transitioned from disappointment to fury when the realization struck that she was powerless.

"You fools!" she roared, the high pitch of her echoes bouncing off the cave walls, causing me to wince. Dali and Akim reached down into the stairway and grabbed me by the elbow, and I snatched Gavin's with my free hand, Josh quickly tagging along as we were yanked out of the entryway and back into the sunlight.

"You knew about this!" Samira rushed forward to charge us, but an invisible shield tough as iron hit her head on at the doorway, blocking her from exiting, sending her into a new wave of rage.

"Come on, mates! Hurry it up!" Dali pulled us farther back so he could slam the door shut in her face. I heard the hinges begin to groan and I shot forward to jam my hand in the opening before they closed it off.

"Samira," I said forcefully, looking her in the face, "I have no idea what's going on, but you have my word, I'll be back."

The look Gavin gave me in that moment was full of an ungodly amount of disgust, but he swallowed it back and waited for me to finish speaking to her. Thinking he had some nerve, looking at me like that, I pulled back and let Dali and Akim allow the door to shut.

"Care to share what the hell is going on?" Gavin asked them, unleashing a protective stance in front of me.

"Quickly, to the windmill. We'll explain there." Akim turned to leave, but Gavin's arm sprang forward and squeezed him so tightly he cried out in pain.

"Remember that human thing called pain?" Gavin spoke through gritted teeth, leaning in close to his face. "I'll introduce you to it again, and there will be no measure to its end. Everyone and everything I love is within this realm and so help me God, if you do anything to jeopardize their safety any more than I already have, today will be the worst day of your life. The last hundred years you spent in Samira's doghouse will have *nothing* on today, you got that?"

Dali stepped forward and placed his hand on Gavin's forearm. "Easy there, mate. We're not the enemy—she's in the dungeon right now."

"Gav," Josh said, moving closer, "come on, man. Let's see what they have to say."

Gavin searched Akim's face, reluctantly letting go to turn and wrap an arm around my waist. My body stiffened at his touch. "All right, get on with it."

We zipped around the hill and marched up to the windmill, securing the door shut once inside.

"All right, lovely, take that special book of yours out now," Akim said, pointing to my bag. He wanted me to hand over the book? The one I'd worked so hard to protect, to guard with my life? It had guided us to this very place, to this very moment. It was our life raft, the only direction we had at this point. It belonged in my hands.

Remembering that time was of the essence and that Samira was locked up in the haven, I realized I had no other choice. I had to trust whatever it was Dali and Akim had to say. The decision made, I pulled the straps from my shoulder and opened the flap, revealing the Book of the Ancients. Gavin opened his own bag and handed me a pack of blood so I could refuel. I gladly accepted, downing it in one gulp before handing the book over to Akim. Even then my fingers gripped the edges, unable to relinquish it. His hand hovered sternly over the cover.

"You can let go now," he said.

I released it.

"Samira can't leave the haven," he said. "Our magic forbids it. We placed a barrier spell on the place shortly after Gérard created Amaranth. We'd discovered the Amaranthians were keeping the place hidden, and it gave us the perfect advantage over Gérard and Samira: knowledge that their kingdom's people were using the space to meet up and plot against their rule. Not long after we stumbled upon their secret, we decided to use it as a location for trapping Samira when the time was right."

Josh's eyebrows rose. "When the time was right? You mean you were planning to trap her back then?"

"Not exactly," Akim replied, opening the Book of the Ancients. He flipped to the last page, eyes zoning in on the lifeless sketch of Samira and me, the one with the fire intertwined between the span of our fingers. I shifted nervously at the reminder that no one else had seen the illustration yet, only Samira and me. Akim's chin shot up and he deadpanned me, the muscles along his jaw clenching then releasing.

When he couldn't seem to find his words, his friend spoke up for him. "It was more of a backup plan, to detain her and drain the city," Dali said, moving to stand next to him. "In case things got out of hand. We'd seen how the creation of this place changed Gérard. How it changed Samira, too. His greed for power consumed him, and her bitterness was born when she realized he valued this place more than her. Then came the affair, and Arianna's eighteenth birthday, and well … everything went south after that. We'd seen it coming, just as your father had," he looked to Gavin while sitting down on a stack of hay. "Sean was a good man. He sensed the shift in Gérard, knew he was turning to the dark side."

Akim found his voice again. "Sadly, we were a bit too late to do anything about it. The last thing we remember was Samira, in the castle, seizing us with her magic, threatening Gérard, warning him to release her from the Amaranth realm so she could return to earth. He saw she'd frozen us under her magic, but he reached the doorway and just laughed, then strolled away. No remorse for abandoning her … or us." His hands began shaking in anger as he relived the moment his magic and free will were stripped from him, when one of his supposed best friends left him to suffer without a second thought. I extended a hand to console him.

"So what's the answer?" I asked. "What do we have to do to end this?"

Dali crossed his arms and inhaled sharply, his gaze holding mine. "Three things cement Gérard's power: fire, a drop of loyal blood, and a sacrifice. He needed all three to create it, and the same three elements can destroy it."

"Okay," Gavin said and straightened, cracking his knuckles. "What kind of fire, blood, and sacrifice are we talking here?"

"He used a circle of fire—created by a designated

firestarter," Dali's eyes shot to mine, then to Gavin, "a drop of loyal blood, which came from Erica, and a sacrifice: banning Samira to the exile as gatekeeper. At one point in time, his love for her was true.... It really was a sacrifice for him to banish her here for eternity."

Gavin, Josh, and I all began spewing questions at once; Dali and Akim's voices were drowned out by our rambling. We realized talking over one another wasn't getting us anywhere, so we shut up.

Gavin went first. "You said a drop of loyal blood, from my mother. What did she have to do with this?"

Dali pointed to my necklace, once Erica's necklace. "One of the ingredients needed for the spell that would secure his control as a hybrid was right under his fingertips: a drop of loyal blood." Leveling his gaze with Gavin, his expression was full of empathy. "He admired your parents' relationship, saw how devoted they were to one another. He knew your mother would do anything—give anything—to protect your father. So he presented a false protection spell to them one night under the guise of friendship, convincing them it would be cast to protect their love always. He took a drop of your mother's blood, but instead he used it to secure his power as creator of Amaranth. Erica was the key. Without her, the spell couldn't be complete. Her heart was loyal to the core. It was easy for Gérard to pull one over on your father, because your father was still new to the conjure world then, was learning to practice magic under Gérard's instruction."

Akim stepped closer to continue for his friend, eyeing my necklace as he spoke. "You see, long before Gérard created this realm, he'd been planning to secure power over the witches: experimenting with Samira's hybrid qualities, creating and revising spells, trying new conjure techniques. In the beginning, he was a witch first and foremost. Later, he created the vampire curse. You were quite young at the time. He was the one who turned your parents into frozen souls."

Josh gasped and I clutched my chest at hearing this, but Gavin didn't move, didn't blink.

Akim started to pace, his hands flailing while he revealed the missing pieces, the parts of the witches' and vampires' history upon which we desperately needed light shed. "When the vampires were created, the witches weren't immediate enemies with them. They disapproved, had resented that Gérard used their magic to create the frozen souls, but they were civil at first. The witches simply saw the creation as an experiment and nothing more. They didn't realize what he intended to do with it. We—including your father—were the first frozen souls to begin meshing the witches' magic with our curse's powers, and for a while, it was harmless. When Gérard discovered the kind of power he had as a hybrid, he changed his tune. Suddenly, he didn't want the frozen souls to know they could use the witches' magic amongst their kind."

"Yes," Dali agreed, scanning the windmill's floor as if searching for and retrieving the memories for himself.

"That's when the real trouble began," he said. "When he started using his hybrid creation for his benefit, coming up with the idea to create Amaranth, to use it as a fulltime energy source. That's when everything changed between the original witches and the frozen souls."

"A perversion," I whispered, recalling Vivienne's retelling of the witches' expulsion of the vampires.

"Yes. They saw how Gérard misused their magic, and they immediately lost respect for him ... then started to fear him."

"So were you both ... hybrids as well?" I asked.

"Not quite. Gérard made sure that didn't happen. We were linked to his magic when we began practicing with one another, so our powers were just as strong as any original witch's. Once we knew about the hybrid abilities, though, Gérard started distancing himself from us ... I don't doubt that's why he left us the way he did."

Gavin was in a trance now, his gaze set somewhere past Dali and Akim's shoulders. Wherever he was, he definitely wasn't in this windmill. My fingers found my necklace's locket, my visions of Erica's room, the skeleton key that unlocked it, and the significance of it all coming into clear view now.

Josh ran a hand through his hair and began pacing like Akim, which made me want to do more than pace. I wanted to run. Fly, then run, and run some more. "So you're saying we need Erica's blood again to break the spell?" Josh asked. "Well that should be easy then, right, Gav? She's here, she's alive—"

Dali and Akim's faces lit up. "Erica's alive?"

"Yeah," I answered. "Samira decided to keep her around."

Gavin returned from his trance abruptly, adjusting his backpack and cracking his knuckles again, his nostrils flaring. Shoving one hand in his pocket, he slipped an arm around my waist and ignored their questions. "So, Gérard had a drop of loyal blood, and a sacrifice." He spat out the words. Then he said, "Well, who was the firestarter?"

"You were," Dali said softly. "You don't remember."

"I'm pretty sure I'd remember something like that."

Dali nodded, and Akim looked to him, as if to offer his condolences for being a bearer of such bad news. "One night while you were out with your friends, Gérard found you and pulled you aside. He used mind compulsion to lure you into Amaranth for the ritual."

Gavin's jaw ticked and he shook his head slowly, his anger visibly festering beneath his trembling frame. "Well, that's just wonderful. So let's reverse the damn thing and be done with it. I've had enough lies!" He stepped away from me, lunging forward to take Dali and Akim by the scruffs of their necks. "Do you hear me? This is over! All of it. Right now."

"Gavin!" I screeched, Josh surging forward with me to pull Gavin off them.

"Gav, take it easy, man, they're trying to help!" Josh said.

"Help?" Gavin shouted. "They sat back and watched

all of this happen, from the beginning." He shot the men another menacing look. "You watched Gérard use, lie to and destroy my family, under the guise of family friends! Not to mention the countless other lives here and on earth, all ruined because of that bastard. I'll make damn sure you get everything you deserve when this is over."

I wanted to scream, *Gavin, don't burn this bridge just yet. We need these guys to tell us how to complete the spell!* But the words wouldn't come. My heart and insides were completely leveled by the betrayal and hurt on his face, even after the betrayal he'd inflicted on me, because damn it, I loved him anyway. All of his pain was overshadowed by the anger, but I could see it, could feel it there, simmering just beneath the surface, and it was a god-awful feeling I could relate to. It was the feeling I'd had every time I'd realized I'd welcomed yet another toxic relationship into my life, each time I'd sold a piece of my dignity to the highest bidder. And it was the feeling that consumed me when I'd faced the harsh reality that once again, my addict mother had disappointed me. That she wasn't and couldn't ever be reliable, no matter how many times I placed my trust in her. She'd simply pick it up and shatter it into a million pieces over and over again, resulting in the same raw affliction that now dressed Gavin's face.

He was in no condition to finish this conversation, and he was about to pulverize our only connections to the key that would end Gérard and Samira's kingdom once and for all. As angry as I was with him for how he went about this mission, one truth remained: He wanted justice, and I couldn't fault him for that.

I swallowed and staggered forward to Dali and Akim with a deep breath. "He's upset. Please show us how to cast the spell. You need me to get a drop of Erica's blood? Okay, done. What else do you need? I'll do it. I'll do anything. *Please*."

Akim crossed his arms, hesitating, and behind me I could hear Josh trying to calm Gavin down. "It doesn't work that way," Akim finally said. "The same elements will destroy Gérard, but the spell must be recreated."

"Okay, so what?"

"Well, for starters ..." He returned the Book of the Ancients to me, pointing to the last illustrated page. "If the ancients are leading us in the right direction, it looks as if you're the firestarter this time."

My eyes landed on the page. I stared hard at it, willing it to tell me otherwise.

No such luck.

Gavin and Josh appeared by my side, Gavin's voice cooler than before, but still bitter. "What about the blood and the sacrifice?"

"You are the ones casting the spell. Only time will tell."

"What the hell kind of vague answer is that? Gérard *planned* the original spell. He had designated players all lined up. Why aren't the ancients giving us *those* answers?" Gavin smacked the page. "Why isn't this thing lighting up to tell us who should do what?"

"What I mean is, you will have to choose who plays which role in the ritual. The book reveals truths as it's destined to. That's always how it's worked. When the time comes, it will confirm whether you're on the right path. In our day, it revealed wisdom for the witches: how to live, the meaning of life, those sorts of things. This prophecy we're dealing with is new. We know as much about it as you do, if not less."

"Yeah," Dali chimed in. "We've been wolves for the last few decades, remember? We're not exactly in the loop."

Akim nodded, his eyebrows pulling together in thought. "And there's still one other thing we need to figure out."

Josh reached over and closed the Book of the Ancients, took it from my hand and placed it into my backpack. Words were still dead on my lips.

"Which is?" Gavin asked.

"Why Gérard hasn't come for us yet. And why he let Camille come to us when he knows we hold the secret to his destruction—"

The wooden latch clicked on the windmill door and we all turned to face the intruder, Josh, Gavin, and I instantly drawing our knives when it creaked open.

"I think I can answer that for you," Scarlet cooed, withdrawing a knife of her own from her inner thigh, just below the hem of her dress. She bared her fangs and shot forward, heading straight for Dali and Akim. Josh lurched behind me to whisk Dali and Akim out of the way, and before Gavin could, I collided with her. In a moment of supreme glory, our eyes met and I plunged my silver dagger straight into her heart.

10

SIREN

"Camille!" Gavin shouted from behind me. Scarlet looked down at the dagger and then back up at me, a euphoric smile spreading across her face. I glanced down at my fingers in shock. They were wrapped tightly around the dagger's handle, the end of the blade shoved deep into her chest. Seeing no smoke radiate from her chest and hearing no burning flesh, I stumbled back, waiting for her to drop or cry out. Instead, she laughed and shoved me back farther, straight into Gavin's arms, yanking the dagger from her heart with vigor. She'd found a way to enhance her protection spell—the one Vivienne helped us cast—the last time we were here, in Amaranth, managing to evade us after she destroyed our mission. Was the same spell protecting her now? How had she kept it intact since then?

My mind was spinning, but my reflexes swiftly caught up with my racing thoughts. I charged forward and slammed into her again, running her straight into the windmill's brick wall. Gavin launched toward her next, coming at her from the side, but she thrust her hand into the air as I held her by the throat and swirled her wrist, just as Samira did, and Gavin flew back, landing in a stack of hay.

Tightening my grip on her throat, I bared my fangs and dug my fingers into her skin. She hissed and threw all of her force into one shove, pushing off the wall and tackling me onto the ground, landing astride me and pinning me by the throat. She peered down, a cougar ready to dig into her prey, and Gavin came at her again. She broke eye contact with me and glanced up at him as he soared through the air, zapping him clear across the space and this time, nailing him to the wall. I pressed my head back against the floor to watch him smack into the room's brick interior.

"Ahhhhh!" he roared, realizing he couldn't move his hands or feet. My eyes darted around the room, desperate to find Josh, Dali and Akim, but I couldn't see them anywhere.

"I have a few tricks of my own now, Camille," she said as she returned her triumphant smile to me, gazing down as if she held the power of a thousand suns beneath her grasp. "And I'm only going to get stronger." The heady look frightened me, and I knew I had to think fast. My jaw clenched as I swiveled my hip to the side to twist and buck her off me, freeing up just enough room to bump her and cause her to lose her grasp of one of my wrists. I took full advantage, and delivered a punch across her face and then threw my forehead forward to punch her squarely in the nose. She fell back and I sprang to my feet, turning to find Gavin had slumped to the floor.

Scarlet stumbled as she stood, glaring at him as she directed her hand in the air to control him. His body raised slightly off the ground but then dropped, and the frustration was written over her face. She gave up as the power unraveled before her and weakened, letting her arm fall back to her side. Snatching her dagger instead, she lunged toward me again and spun me around, relying on her physical strength to position me into a headlock.

She held the knife to my throat as she backed up toward the windmill door, and Gavin inched forward, hands in the air. "What is it you want, Scarlet?" he asked.

"I already have what I want right here."

"Let her go."

"Ha." Against my back, her body shook with laughter. "*Tu es très drôle.* Why don't you run along and find your coward friends? So sorry things didn't work out between us, but I suppose we had a good run while it lasted, right baby?"

I struggled against her grip, but the edge of her blade skimmed the skin of my throat and I shrieked in pain, the smoke drifting up and into my nostrils. Gavin started forward again, but Scarlet's power, weak as it was now, slowed him. His steps were quicksand, each one a struggle.

"*Ah-ah-ah,* " she said, using her free hand to hold it vertical in front of me. It was shaking, as if it was warring with some unseen force, and I could feel her struggle to maintain the power she was using to control him. Pulling me tighter against her chest, she wrenched me to the left and turned us to the door to exit.

"Camille!" Gavin's scream echoed from inside the windmill, but we were gone.

Scarlet loosened her grip on me just a hair, keeping her dagger tight and close to my collarbone, guiding me forward, down the hill and into the valley. My limbs wanted me to run, my mind urging me to fight back and break from her grip while I had a chance, knowing nothing good awaited me wherever she was planning to take me. With one glance at the shiny silver flashing near my neck and the images of what just went down in the windmill replaying in my mind, that desire was frozen in fear.

How had she acquired this kind of power? Had she known more about the witches' magic all along, more than she originally let on? Or had she learned from Gérard himself all those years ago, and found a way to use it to her advantage now? I couldn't wrap my brain around any of it. All I knew was I had to extract information from her, and that talking to her was likely my only chance of escape. Wherever Josh, Dali, and Akim were now, there was hope that Gavin would find them and that they'd come for me soon. If only he could move.

"Why won't you just tell us what you want, Scarlet?" I asked. "Do you want Gavin? Well go ahead, I'm not standing in your way anymore. He and I are done."

Scarlet slid me a side-glance, the corner of her lips

giving away a hint of amusement. "You're a terrible liar, Camille. But that's okay. You're also a masochistic fool, which makes you the perfect candidate for running around saving everyone else at the cost of your own suffering. You're always more than willing to volunteer, aren't you?" She jerked my head to the side, enjoying my murderous expression. "You are truly more naive than I gave you credit for. You really think Gavin is what I'm after? That my goal would be that shortsighted? Ha! Sure, I wanted him at first. The last time we were here I made that clear, but you didn't comply, and I warned him you would pay. But that was only because I was hoping I could have them both in my new kingdom. Gérard is … well, he's just delicious. But he'll be gone often, doing God knows what, and I'll need a king. Someone who can satisfy my whims. And Gavin *certainly* knows how to satisfy a woman."

"What … what are you talking about?"

She ignored my question.

"Gavin chose to reject me. So be it. I'll be perfectly content reigning on my own, and there will be plenty to keep me satisfied."

She continued to guide me down into the valley toward the village, and I grew more frantic, desperate to see Dali, Akim, Josh or Gavin—anyone—before she dragged me somewhere out of sight and I lost any chance of being found. I said, "Where are you taking me?"

A dark laugh sounded from deep in her throat, and once again, she avoided my question. "All this time I thought Gavin found you appealing because he felt sorry for you, but it's clearer now. You're completely disposable. Pliable and convenient, just the way he likes it. He might have had fun with the chase, but that thrill will be gone soon, you'll see. In the end, you'll be nothing to him, and he'll still be the same old Gavin I knew him to be: carnal, impulsive, and on to the next chase."

My teeth began to grind as I worked to restrain my rage, aware my temper could take this situation from horribly bad to worse. The main village grew closer and closer as the steep decline of the windmill's hill began to level out, and I couldn't hold back. "I think you're confusing me with someone," I spat through gritted teeth.

"Is that so?"

"Yeah, *you*."

Her eyes flashed liquid venom and she jerked us to a stop at the edge of the village's main street. "What did you just say?"

"Gérard had fun with you, and then threw you out with the trash. Looks to me as if you're the disposable one."

Obviously, the wrong thing to say.

Her silver dagger collided with my torso, and as it sank into my flesh, I rejoiced in the fact that I'd hit my target, even if it meant paying for it. She watched me hit the ground with a thud and I writhed in agony at her feet, the smoke from the metal's contact with my skin sizzling so loudly, I could barely make out her words as she hovered above me.

Seeming to sense this, she crouched down to speak close to my ear. "Apparently, not so disposable, because soon, Samira's throne will be mine. You? You are *nothing.* Just a weak, pitiful excuse for a frozen soul. I should have ended you while I had the chance."

Gasping, I curled into a fetal position and clutched the dagger's handle, pulling it from my stomach and chucking it on the ground. "What's … stopping you?"

She leaned in closer, her eyes dark coal, and picked up the dagger again, slicing it across my arm. "Because I need this," she said, watching the blood drip down my arm and into the dirt. She kept one hand firmly on my throat while she dropped the dagger and pulled a clear vial, attached to a necklace, from her bra. She unscrewed the vial's cap and tipped the tube to the stream of blood running down my arm, watching it fill. "Your sad, loyal blood. If I'm to reign as the new queen, Samira needs to be relieved of her duty first. The spell to break her power and transfer it to another requires the loyalist of blood to be taken and sacrificed in this realm. Gérard needed you here, alive—at least until the ritual is complete. Why else do you think he kept you around?"

She finished filling the vial and screwed the cap back on, holding it up to admire her work. "He knew your blood was the key, that you'd be the only one who'd sacrifice anything for your imbecile friends: You'd even save Samira! None of the others would do such a thing. He was going to bring you through the portal himself to perform the ritual, before those blasted witches got in his way. Isn't it funny?" She smiled once more at the necklace, then slipped it over her head; the vial of blood dangled from her neck. "Loyalty being the price for betrayal?"

The piercing strain the dagger's blade had left in the pit of my stomach began to spread, paralyzing my limbs and weighing me to the ground, my mobility lessening by the second.

This shouldn't be happening, but it was.

All of it pointed to injustice, an abuse of power, an unnatural order of things. Good was supposed to triumph over evil, not the other way around. Destroying the enemy wasn't supposed to be this hard. An army of good confronting the darkness should've caused its foundation to crumble by now, but instead, the light was being crushed beneath its feet.

As I lay there in the dirt, my consciousness fading while Scarlet rose to her feet above me, Joel's words drifted through my mind: *Where is the victory without opposition?* I'd believed those words before, and I'd be damned if I was going to give up on them, even now.

I released one last battle cry, arching my back off the ground, allowing all my grief to pour from my lips. It bellowed from deep in my stomach and the depths of my soul, the wail piercing my ears as I willed my friends to hear me. Somewhere, they had to hear me. The village's street was too quiet, everything deserted, the wind too still. Where did they go? Did they join the frontlines to retrieve help?

Scarlet stood over me, staring down in satisfaction. "Aw, are you hoping your friends will come for you?" Her bitter laugh cut through me, and I could feel her crouch down again, the slide of the blade audible at my ear as she dragged it through the dirt. She picked it up and gripped it firmly, her voice beside me, breath hot on my cheek. "Well don't waste your breath. They're all dead."

"No!" I refused to listen, rejected her words and forced them to flee. "I don't believe you."

"No?" The ground began to shake and a tumultuous thundering raged in the distance, calling her attention toward Samira's cathedral on the hill, her eyes scanning the gates. She snapped her head back to me, and she was beaming. "See for yourself."

She tilted my head to align my vision with the bottom of the cathedral's hill, and my gaze climbed the valley's incline and landed on the gates at the very top, where packs of marching bodies joined together in formation.

"No!" I cried out. "No! What have you done?" Audrey, Gabe and Arianna. No, they couldn't be gone. They *couldn't*. Gavin and Josh were just with me in the windmill. They didn't go to join the others. They wouldn't—not without coming for me first. *Damn it!* Why did Dali and Akim have to lock Samira up like that? Why were the streets deserted? My friends couldn't have survived an army of that size at the frontlines.

"I guess that's my cue," Scarlet said, and gripped the

dagger tighter between both hands. "As soon as the ritual is complete, you'll no longer be needed. In the meantime … I'd be cruel to let you miss the show." Winking down at me, she raised her arms and slammed down, plunging the knife into my stomach again, drawing another fierce scream from my lips. All hopes of regaining a shred of mobility were lost when the silver struck; the paralyzing effect planted an even deeper seed as it lodged deep. I could barely lift my chin, let alone my fingers or feet.

Scarlet sprang to her feet and flew off toward the gates, and the thundering continued to roar, the ground beneath me vibrating to the march of the enemy's beating drum.

"Camille!" My eyelids fluttered at the sound as it came from behind me, the voice strained and distant. "Camille, can you hear me?"

"Gavin?" I croaked, pushing out my voice as hard as I could. Where was he? He sounded so far away. My vision began to blur.

"Camille, the book!" His voice grew closer, and so did the sound of the marching. A warmth was beginning to spread beneath me, a soft, rattling humming against my back. "The Book of the Ancients!" I listened as his voice grew louder, more pronounced, and then felt light all around me. My eyes widened and I could see the light—golden, blinding light. Finally, a shadow loomed over me, and the voice was now clear. "Baby, I'm here." He moved to lift me up into his arms, stumbling at first. He kissed every inch of my face, tears and sweat on his cheeks.

"What's wrong?" My voice cracked, the paralysis making it difficult to speak.

"I'm still having a hard time moving. It took me forever to get down this hill. I don't know what the hell she did to me up in the windmill."

"She's ... taking *overrrr*."

"What, baby?" He leaned in closer, yanking the dagger from my flesh. "You're too weak. The paralysis will wear off in a bit. We have to move." He rolled me to the left and pulled the Book of the Ancients from my bag, which was still attached to my back. It was glowing so brightly, I had to squint to look at it. Stuffing it underneath his arm, he scooped me up and cradled me against his chest, then started back uphill, toward the windmill.

"They're getting close," I choked out as he carried me. He'd stumble every few seconds, stopping to steady himself.

"I know."

We made it to the windmill door and he managed to pull it open, laying me down on some hay before locking it shut behind us. I worked to stretch my fingers, but still no movement yet. He set the Book of the Ancients down and flipped it open, cursing under his breath. The glowing was diminishing, but still bright enough to light up our surroundings. "There's nothing shown on the next page," he said. "It's lighting up, but it's still blank, I don't understand—"

"Where's Josh?"

"He's okay, he's down below with Dali and Akim. Come on." He snapped the book shut and scooped me back up, carrying me to the far corner of the windmill. I remembered this space from our wedding night, and our secret rendezvous when we'd had to hide our meetings from Scarlet.

"Look what Dali and Akim had buried away." He gestured to a straw-covered patch on the floor. Bending down, he felt for a latch and pulled. A large door swung open to reveal an underground crawlspace.

"We found it, mate!" Dali's voice carried upward from the hole and into the windmill. Gavin carried me down into the space, the book's golden light further illuminating the area around us, which was already lit with an array of lanterns. Josh lay unconscious on a long wooden plank that had been propped up like a table atop some large stones, his arm cut at the elbow. No wonder none of them had come for me.

"Josh's been passed out for Dali and Akim's ritual," Gavin said, setting me down. "While I was stuck up in the windmill, they've been trying to forage through their old stuff to recreate a spell that can give them their power back."

"They can do that?"

"We're trying," Akim answered, shaking a potion and handing it to Dali. "No guarantees how strong we'll be, but it's worth a shot." They busied themselves around a small shelf, studying a stack of papers and reading aloud ingredients and instructions of some sort to one another. The shelf was full of colorful bottles and dusty jars. I didn't want to know what was in them.

I attempted to force more words out while Gavin cracked open the Book of the Ancients again, flipping through pages like a maniac. I managed to say, "Scarlet is taking over."

Gavin's head snapped in my direction, and Dali dropped a potion that Akim caught before it shattered on the floor. "What?" they asked in unison.

"She needed my blood. Said something about Gérard needing me alive in this realm for his spell to work. A spell that will transfer Samira's power over to her. Said everyone at the frontlines was dead." That last thought caused more tears to spill over my cheeks; the idea that all our friends were gone was unbearable when we'd come this far.

Dali glanced to Akim, eyes wide. "Hurry, mate." He didn't have to ask again. Akim moved faster. Outside the space, I could sense the marching getting closer, the ground's vibrations growing more persistent. Gavin must have sensed it too; his expression hardened, his gaze moving over my immobile form, then settling somewhere far off, the haunted look in his eyes distressing to witness. He seemed to snap out of it when he realized I was no longer speaking, and then, he too moved faster. The dagger's paralyzing effect had taken over my ability to say more, and I'd never felt more helpless in my life.

"Come on!" he yelled at the book, flipping to the back again. "Just give me something, damn it!" Dali and Akim began chanting, clasping hands over Josh as they did. A whipping gust of wind zipped around us and then stilled, the lanterns and the Book of the Ancients' light dying as Dali and Akim's chants halted. Everything went black then, and the crawlspace became eerily quiet except for the echoes of the army's marching outside. It shook the ground above, curtains of dirt and dust showering us as the pulsing sent tremors through our bones.

"They're here," Gavin whispered in the dark.

The marching ceased and I immediately missed its sound.

The door latch made a slamming noise above us and the door flung open, casting light down into the dark space. The lanterns' flames flickered until they resumed their full glow. Dali and Akim's bodies stood tall and still as stone, eyes opened but no life in them.

Akim breathed first—fast and sharp, a breath of life. Then came Dali's movement, gasping as if he'd been held under water far too long. They both extended their arms, first stretching their fingers and then their necks. Heads rolling backward, their gazes met the light above. Turning, they slowly shifted to face Gavin, and Gavin stepped back to position himself in front of me. He drew his blade, stance cautious.

Dali blinked, stance just as guarded, and an invisible force wrenched Gavin's dagger away, sending it straight to Dali's open palm. He gripped it tight, a relieved smile curling on his lips, but he didn't hang onto it for long. The same force returned the knife to Gavin's grip, and

Dali's shoulders relaxed. The relief that Dali had restored his power registered on Akim's face, too, and everyone released the breath they'd been holding. Josh groaned as he awoke and sat up on the improvised table. He rubbed his eyes and looked around, voice groggy. "Gav? Is everything okay?"

Gavin didn't have time to respond, because the Book of the Ancients blinded us, its light returning full force, and with it, my limbs began to move. A cough escaped my throat and my body was quicker than my mind, hopping up from the ground and stretching, immediately joining Gavin, Dali and Akim as they gathered to study the book's illustration. Gavin helped me stand, and I worked hard to focus on the page and not the mayhem that waited outside, or the fact that my mobility was restored—which was hard, because my God, being able to walk and move had never felt so good.

Focus was easy when I spotted the words as they appeared in fancy, old-world script on the last page. Their presence was a siren, calling to me:

A firestarter to commence our fate
A drop of loyal blood before it's too late
A sacrifice of will awaits
The last one standing behind the gates

II

LOYALTY

"That's your cue, Camille," Dali said, reaching for more silver daggers from the shelf. He handed them to us so we were now armed with two each, then shoved the Book of the Ancients into my backpack and slipped it over my arms. No one else said a word, didn't bother to decode the words revealed to us, because we knew.

This was everything we'd been waiting for, and there wasn't a second more to lose. The army—whatever army Gérard had prepared for us—was just outside the windmill, and no matter how many or few of our friends and Amaranthians remained, they were depending on us.

"It's time to go, mates," Akim said, leading the way up the ladder and out of the bunker.

Josh and Dali followed him, and Gavin came to my side. I froze. "Wait."

Dali and Akim swung around, Dali already halfway up the ladder. "What is it?"

"You have to release Samira from the haven."

"That's out of the question."

"Hey," I took a step forward, "do you want me to start the fire or not? I need her. The book showed me, you saw it for yourself."

Gavin spoke up. "I still don't trust her, Camille. I don't care what that picture showed you, she could turn on us and—"

"She's right," Akim murmured, gaze lowering to the ground, then up to Dali. "I'll take care of it. The rest of you go, buy us some time until the book tells us what to do next. I won't let anything happen to her, Gavin."

Dali, Josh and Akim started up the ladder, and Gavin lassoed me back, tucking us into a dark corner of the bunker, my back to the cool wall. He peered down at me, his eyes a blazing, mocha elixir. Without a word, he angled his head, lips hesitating at mine as he closed his eyes. His chest rose and fell against mine, and I reached up and ran a thumb over his forehead's crescent scar, searching for his gaze in the dim light, imploring him to trust me, and to know I forgave him for … everything. It all seemed so petty in the grand scheme of things now, and I was certain whatever we were about to face would further clarify our true priorities. Love couldn't be moved by circumstance, poor choices, or even blatant lies—skewed and damaged, yes, but the heart couldn't deny what it wanted most once the desire was planted. Whether in bliss or affliction, love owned you all the same.

That shy smile I loved so much formed on his lips, and his eyes fluttered opened. This was the Gavin I missed: vulnerable, raw, and affectionate. It was so … human. A rare sight since he'd been forced to claim the role of our mission's leader. He responded to my touch, bringing the pad of his thumb to the corner of my shirt hem, inching it up and then smoothing it down onto my hip's matching crescent scar, mimicking the same soothing motion. We stood there, scar to scar, skin to skin, forehead to forehead, our bodies saying everything we couldn't. He shifted his mouth and captured my lips, pressing me tight against the wall until he kissed the breath right out of me.

"Get my blood from Scarlet," I whispered when he pulled back. "It's in a vial around her neck."

"I'll do what I can. You and Akim focus on completing that spell." His lips found my forehead and then he released me, turning for the ladder after our friends. I followed and ascended into the windmill, where we gathered around the door and opened the heavy wood latch.

The door opened and everything I'd witnessed last time, in this very spot, paled in what lay before us now. In the valley below, the Amaranthian villages were leveled, only the cobblestone streets and scattered, flattened beds of debris remaining.

And then there were the bodies.

"My God," I choked out, my forearm flying over my mouth to cover my gasp. Through the tears and the distance, I could make out every face, every ghastly expression there in the street, trampled and destroyed beneath the formations of frozen souls that filled every inch of the village. Women clinging to one another, men grasping the stones of the street with bloodied, withered fingers, faces down in the dirt as if they'd been dragging themselves across it. Was there anyone left to save? Had this entire mission been in vain? My mind slammed me with the grief, sending spiraling waves of guilt to my core: We'd brought this upon them.

The blood and destruction was so overwhelming, I almost missed the other eyesore clear across the valley, at the top of the cathedral's hill. The gates had been demolished, an opening that seemed the size of a continent bulldozed through the surrounding fortress walls.

"There," Gavin said, voice low, eyes zoning in on movement amidst the center of the army's formation. A bold red and a flash of milky skin appeared between the shoulders of the guards, rippling the formation with vivid distinction. Its vivacious pop contrasted with the black-and-gray hooded cloaks the guards wore, and it was moving toward the bottom of the hill, in our direction.

Scarlet.

Exchanging glances with Josh, Dali, Akim and me, Gavin raised his knives and crouched forward, ready to charge down the hill and into the valley. "Now!" His voice was a bomb, detonating the deceptive silence around us, and as he, Josh and Dali flew forward, Akim and I darted to the right and down the back side of the hill toward the haven. One glance over my shoulder chilled me.

Their heads disappeared down the hill's slope, and that knowledge propelled me forward with so much vigor, for the first time, I was truly afraid of my own strength.

We reached the haven and descended into its cave. Samira rushed forward to meet us at the bottom of the stairwell, her face grave, eyes piercing Akim with unprecedented malice.

She turned her gaze on me, moving closer and holding out a hand, her first balled tight. The Book of the Ancients brightened from behind me, lighting up the cave while Akim dashed to a nearby table to pull potions and herbs from his bag.

"Samira?" I stepped closer to get a good look at her hand. She searched my face and uncurled her fist, holding out her palm. I gripped her wrist, and my eyes shot up to hers when I spotted the box of matches. Not breaking our contact, I slipped my bag off my shoulder with one hand and pulled out the Book of the Ancients. Its cover blasted opened and revealed the last page, the same illustration we'd seen before, of a luminescent stream of fire passing between her fingertips and mine. We both gasped in realization that the book was indeed giving us our cue. Stunned, Samira dropped the matches. I scooped them up and stumbled backward until my heels hit the bottom of the stairwell.

"Samira!" Akim shouted, calling her to the table. She turned to him but her anger with him was lost, just as mine was with Gavin. Her eyes were wide in shock and jaw slack at what had just passed between us.

"It's all really happening," she murmured to herself.

"Yes," Akim surged forward and grabbed her hand, "it is. Now you can get over here, link me to your magic, and fight with us, or rot in this hole by yourself. What's it going to be?"

"What? I—"

Waves of shouting and thunder shook the ground above us and we winced.

"Now!" Akim said. "I won't break the barrier and let you out unless you link me first. What's it going to be?" Not waiting for her to make the call, he grabbed a silver pin, unrolled some parchment and began to read the words aloud, chanting and reciting them as he went, Samira's indecision bouncing between my gaze and his. Between chants, he shouted, "Damn it, Camille, you have the matches, now go!"

"But I don't know what to do with them yet!"

He pointed to the Book of the Ancients while he popped open a bottle of potion to pour it into a bowl, his shaky hands knocking over a rack of bottles on the table as he worked.

I turned and clutched the edges of the book, scanning the pages until I landed on the golden, swirling light as it illuminated the page next to the final message.

A firestarter to commence our fate.

The picture came to life, a ring of fire encasing Gérard, and I immediately recognized the cathedral's throne room. My gaze lifted to Akim and he nodded fiercely.

"Go!" he shouted again, pulling tighter on Samira's

wrist.

I flew forward and seized Samira's shoulders. "Do it, Samira. Please! We need your magic, *please*!"

The booming uproar above us quaked, and I jetted to the stairwell without a second glance and ascended from the cave's depths and into the overcast sunlight, shoving the matchbox into my pocket as I did. Shooting up from the ground into flight, I flew over the back side of the hill and landed next to the windmill, gazing down into the valley's chaos. My friends were in combat, Dali blasting his magic toward the rows of guards as they surged toward him, Gavin and Josh to his left, all protected by what seemed to be an orb of light, its halo highlighting a perimeter around their feet. Frozen souls darted toward them, yet Gavin and Josh's knives collided with their chests before the enemy could strike or restrain them.

With a deep breath and a final glance at my target, the cathedral on the opposite side of the valley, I rocketed into the air and bolted clear across my friends and the army below. I landed just in front of the pile of rubble near the gates, stepping over the golden bars and toward the castle. Slinking around the cathedral's rear walls, I slipped past the wooden doors and through the back corridor, only a trickling of guards making their way toward Amaranth's entrance as I slithered by. My entire body was in tune with the Book of the Ancients' energy as it hummed in my backpack, and I waited to feel its familiar warmth and connect with its light.

Approaching Samira's throne room doors, I glanced

from left to right, noting the hallway's unnatural emptiness. I entered and floated toward the center of the room; the fireplace crackled, its light shedding a radiant glow on the stone floor. I swallowed hard and readjusted the silver knives in my hand, creeping toward the altar in search of an oil lamp or lantern, something to help start the fire. How I was supposed to manage a circle of fire with Gérard smack in the middle of it was beyond me, but my feet continued to carry me forward until a sensual chuckle emanated around me and halted my mission.

I spun around but found nothing, only the echoes of the same laugh crawling over and through me, a light breeze whipping at my hair as it moved. The main throne room doors swung wide, and a tired dragging sound rustled from the hall. One body appeared, then two, then three ... until an entire line of bodies hobbled in, their knees disjointed and arms jerking in sporadic, unnatural movements. Their clothing was haggard and torn. Bloody gashes decorated their knees and elbows. Studying their gaunt, pale faces, I realized they weren't just any random bodies—they were the witches from the bayou, those who had turned on Gérard and helped us escape through the portal.

And then I saw their eyes.

The glassy barrenness of them made me stumble back, and suddenly I was studying their bodies again, taking in the greenish-gray tint of their skin, the way their decrepit flesh dangled from their bones around the open wounds. My eyes flashing back to their faces, I realized they were dead.

Just as I was about to doubt a reanimated corpse's ability to do any significant damage, given their slow, decaying condition, their ragged, skeleton-like fingers extended and they reached for one another, linking hands as they did at the bayou. The same smooth, deep chuckle filled the room and I stepped back farther. The witches' mouths moved in unison now, their monotone chants coaxing a wind of some sort, and then a sharp cracking sound from the walls. I jumped and shrieked when the cracks in the stone traveled from the ceiling to the floor like lightning strikes, and as the ground quaked beneath my feet, Gérard appeared at the main entryway and sauntered toward me.

He stepped in front of me, our eyes leveled, and my gaze moved over his face and then downward to roam his naked chest. An enormous cigar rested between his ring-clad fingers, which dangled comfortably at his side, and his feet were bare. His dark gray slacks relaxed in rolled cuffs around his ankles. This time, he wore no hat, revealing buzzed-short hair and a gruesome scar near the top of his hairline.

"Camille," he murmured, a smug smile painting his lips. "We meet again, and perfect timing, might I add." Blowing a puff of smoke to the side, he closed the space between us and traced my hip with his index finger, circling my crescent scar until my insides tingled, his pleased smile intensifying tenfold at my reaction. His mind-compulsion magic was starting to take hold, but every cell in me tried to fight the control. I peered down at his hand as it toyed with my skin, apprising each of his gold rings and the spellbinding symbols they bore, and then my gaze traveled north, over each defined muscle of his stomach and chest, landing on his devilish, succulent lips. Instantly, I wanted to taste them.

I trembled and shook my head, forcing my gaze upward to meet his.

"What is it you intend to do with these?" His fingers skipped over my scar and delved into my pocket, retrieving the box of matches. He held them up, his brows rising in amusement, before he chucked them to the floor. "I'm certain your friends—what's left of them, anyway—are up to no good, so I'll make this short and sweet." He turned and took a drag from his cigar, eyeing the throne room's ceiling as a king would admire his kingdom. "When I warned you not to impart your knowledge of Dali and Akim to the others, I should have known you'd test my challenge. One look at Erica's necklace around your neck, and that vitality in your eyes, and I knew you'd start all sorts of trouble."

He turned to face me again, edging forward, posture carnal and much too enticing. "I sensed your innate sympathy for my ex-wife and realized I'd had a little sacrificial gem right beneath my fingertips. I was hoping you'd accompany me here on your own accord, but you certainly rose to the challenge and pleasantly surprised me." He laughed darkly, reaching over to play with my hair. "You see, I *love* trouble." His head dipped down to find my lips, and the same magnetic pull began to ensnare my senses, my body coming alive at his nearness.

I stepped back, just out of his reach.

"Baby," a voice purred from across the room. "I'm growing impatient, and you know I'm no fun when I'm impatient."

Gérard's expression turned to annoyance, and he twisted in the voice's direction to find Scarlet approaching us from the main entryway, passing the line of witches who now stood stock-still, their eyes glowing an eerie red. The click of her heels grated on each of my nerve endings. She slipped the vial necklace from her neck and strutted over to him, holding it up to let it dangle in midair.

"Ah, yes," he said, taking the necklace from her, "I suppose we have everything we need now."

"Looks like it," she said and grinned, tilting her head to look over his shoulder and straight toward me. Her arms encircled his neck and chest, and her fingers skimmed his collarbone as she leaned into him with a pout. "I'm ready for my kingdom now. I can't *wait* to herd a fresh set of frozen souls into Amaranth and start anew. There aren't many humans remaining to sustain our energy. And besides, it's time for a little renovation, wouldn't you say, baby?"

"Indeed," Gérard muttered, lifting her hands from his neck to drop them to her sides. He stepped away from her and rubbed his chin thoughtfully, then walked to the throne altar to retrieve a handkerchief. "I'm all about renovating. In fact, honey, I believe it's time for quite a few upgrades." He removed the cap from the vial and poured my blood onto the handkerchief, then stuffed it inside a clear bottle. Pouring a splash of a purple-hued potion into it, he corked the bottle and shook it, causing it to bubble up. "Camille, I'd love to make you my new queen, but I doubt your loyal blood would allow you to accept such an offer." He smoothed the altar's linen and rolled open a scroll next, casually studying its text.

My gaze darted to Scarlet. Her expression displayed the same disbelief I felt unravel in my torso at Gérard's admission.

"You … you *what*?" she said, shifting her weight on one hip.

"Oh, I'm sorry," Gérard said, looking up from his task, "did you not hear me the first time? I'd love for Camille to be my new queen." I glanced over my shoulder at the altar, feeling his eyes burning holes into the back of my head as I stood there in shock. "I think we'd have a lot of fun together."

"You—" Scarlet started forward, stopping when Gérard lifted his hand to halt her. "You swore to me … you promised I'd have my place as your queen *ages* ago. What, you're going to toss me out like garbage after all this time? After everything we've been through, every-thing we've planned?" Her hand flew to her hip. "She can't give you anything! She's completely worthless! She's here to *destroy* you!"

"Ah-ah," he replied, returning his attention to the scroll's parchment. "No need to get jealous, honey. I suspected Camille would be less than willing to accept my offer ... and while I do enjoy the idea of compelling her to accept, there would be no satisfaction for me in that decision. I'd much prefer a willing volunteer, which is why I've reserved another option." He snapped his fingers and looked to the entryway. "Isa, come, darling."

Scarlet spun in the direction he called to, her eyes flaring and shoulders tightening when she spotted the tall, statuesque blonde who entered the throne room. The woman's long, flowing white chiffon dress billowed around her legs, and she glided forward as if floating on air. Her angelic golden locks were piled high in a tight bun atop her head, secured with a glistening, diamond-studded headband. Even her eyes, though a bright, entrancing, sapphire blue, sparkled like diamonds.

"Ladies, I'd like you to meet Isadora. She'll be my new queen."

Scarlet gasped, spinning back around to face Gérard. "You ... you *used* me! You bastard!"

"Oh come now, honey." Gérard strolled down the throne steps to stand next to me. Isadora waltzed past Scarlet to join him, taking his hand with a smug smile. "Think of all I've taught you, all the fun we've had. You picked up a few conjure lessons, traveled the world, and now ... helped assist me in building my new kingdom. Now, if you'll excuse me, I have a ritual to attend to, and then Isa and I will be on our way to our new realm once this one is destroyed. The sight of this place is such a bore."

Their new what? I couldn't contain my gasp, and neither could Scarlet.

Her eyes darting around wildly, she began to stutter. "This isn't … no. No, this isn't happening. You couldn't possibly … you *wouldn't!*"

Gérard didn't respond, only positioned himself behind me and slipped an arm around my neck, tipping the potion bottle to his lips to drink. My eyes snapped shut at his nearness and he began to chant in my ear, in a language I couldn't understand and one I was sure I didn't want to.

"No!" Scarlet shrieked, dashing toward him. Isa stepped back in surprise, but Scarlet didn't get far. An invisible shield stopped her before she reached us, and she cried out again, her anger sprouting higher at the obstacle.

My eyes flew open again, frantically scanning the floor for the box of matches. It was too late. Soon Samira's power would be gone. That, I couldn't control. But before Gérard did away with me, I still had a role to play. The book ordained it. I'd have to beat him at his own game.

Scarlet's hollering echoed through the room. She banged tirelessly on the invisible barrier, letting it take the brunt of her rage, and the walls began to crack again, the witches behind her repeating Gérard's chant. He continued to keep me tight beneath his grip, encasing me against his warm, hard chest, and I swallowed, waiting for the right time to dart away and grab the matches. I'd have seconds if I were lucky.

The rear doors were blown open and Dali and Akim blasted into the room, Samira gliding in behind them, her body levitating from the ground. She zoned in on Gérard, then Scarlet, and finally, the woman in white who was now standing patiently at Gérard's side. I squirmed under Gérard's grasp as his chanting grew louder. The walls around us shook and sent clouds of dust around our feet.

Gérard's head snapped in Dali and Akim's direction but he continued to work his magic, his words gaining steam, flowing quicker from his lips. Samira, Dali and Akim were thrown backward, landing flat on their backs, but they recovered instantly, flipping to their feet and joining hands. Shooting gazes in the witches' direction, they began a chant of their own, Samira breaking free from their link to send a blast of light toward them. The witches let loose a unified, shriveled scream, and as it erupted, Samira was once again thrown back and off her feet. Dali and Akim eyed the witches with fierce determination as they struggled to maintain their chant, and a guttural growl began to brew at my ear, breaking through Gérard's words.

The beam of light Samira had directed toward the witches reappeared and Dali and Akim manippulated it with their fingers, locking it on them, and then harnessing and pushing it toward Gérard, causing him to jolt and wail in fury. His arms loosened on me, and I didn't waste the opportunity. I dashed left, where I'd spotted the matchbox, and then leaped to the altar in search of something to start the fire with, my fingers skittering over the table for something, anything.

A glance over my shoulder revealed Samira, Dali and Akim, banded together at the foot of the throne in front of Gérard, still linked to the witches' beam of light, their fingertips shooting the light's rays straight into his chest as they closed in on him. The witches' arms and fingers twitched behind them as Dali, Akim and Samira took over their magic.

My head was about to snap back to the altar when the front doors slammed open and a herd of bodies poured in, a mixture of surviving Amaranthians and an influx of frozen-soul guards, all crashing into the witches' backs, forcing them forward, on Samira's heels. My heart twisted in my chest when I spotted Arianna, Gavin and Josh, charging forward with the crowd, armed with an array of silver daggers. Still no sign of Audrey and Gabe.

The Book of the Ancients warmed my back and I jumped, ripping the backpack from my arms and dragging it out to set it on the altar. The pages flapped violently, revealing the last page, and a golden illustration sprang up and began to paint a near-blinding arrow that pointed toward the rear doors. My gaze shot to them.

Erica, Gabe and Audrey pummeled through the

doorway, and Erica's eyes immediately found mine. Tears pricked my eyelids at the sight of my friends, who I'd thought I'd never see again. Dali, Samira and Akim continued to war with the witches' magic at the front of the throne, and the hordes of bodies that had filled the room were now partaking in one massive brawl, the remaining Amaranthians and members of the resistance grappling with the guards while ghastly apparitions leaked from the cracks in the walls, charging down into the crowd to join the battle.

I backed up against the altar and gripped its sides in terror when the cracks in the walls deepened, unleashing even more spirits from their depths. The ghouls descended into the battle in droves, drifting into bodies of the resistance and possessing them, turning them on their own kind one by one, infusing their pupils with the same red glow that filled the witches' eyes. Isa was cowered behind the throne chair, curled up, chest heaving in panic, and Scarlet, no longer caught behind the invisible barrier Gérard had put in place, dueled with the guards herself, throwing fierce strikes with her dagger. I had no idea who she was fighting for this time, but by the look of vengeance on her face, I guessed it wasn't Gérard.

All of the commotion made for an unnoticed entrance for Erica, Gabe and Audrey, and I struggled to return my gaze to them as they slipped along the back wall and up to the altar to meet me.

Samira's voice broke amidst the room's chaos.

"Camille!" She wrestled the light in one hand and wrenched a small bottle from her corset with the other. "Now!" Pitching the bottle at Gérard's feet, it shattered and released a shiny, oily-looking liquid. With her free hand, she used her magic to spread it into a ring around him, and I flipped open the matchbox and darted down the stairs to reach that circle.

Gérard roared at the sight, and static shocked the rays of light, causing a power bump in Samira, Dali and Akim's magic. The bump resonated all the way to the line of witches behind them, and the witches stumbled back a few feet. Gérard thrust his forearms forward and sent a bomb of magic toward them, blasting them off their feet and farther back, into the heart of the room's combat. He surged forward and lifted Samira from the ground with his power. Fearing what might happen if they came face-to-face, I lit the match and tossed it to the ground.

The circle around him ignited, the flames rising and spreading wildly around the ring, trapping him inside. He shouted and tried to dash through it to reach Samira, but it ricocheted him back, sending him to the ground. I heard my name again and snapped my head around. Erica was rushing down the throne stairs to meet me, the Book of the Ancients in one hand, a dagger in the other. Her hair whipped around her face as she pointed to the illuminated page and I took it from her, studying each line and groove in the illustration.

This time there were words, smooth and simple, lighting up across blots of blood. The blood poured from an image of a shattered bottle and spread and saturated the page, the words still just visible beneath its color: *A drop of loyal blood before it's too late.*

I glanced up to find Erica's eyes locked on mine, her hand dragging her dagger across her palm. Gabe and Audrey rushed up from behind her with a bottle from the altar and she grabbed it, at once filling it with drops of her blood. Before either of us could say a word, she raced down the throne steps and chucked the bottle of blood into the fiery circle, where it smashed next to Gérard's heels. His frenzied eyes widened, and his uproar's vibrations could be felt from the tips of our fingers to the soles of our feet. He charged forward again, attempting to penetrate the fiery barrier, but it was no use.

His power was already diminishing, the evidence scattered across the room.

The apparitions began to fade, their banshee cries screeching in the air as they vanished, and the reanimated witches' bodies sagged to the ground, their eyes' red glow dulling to a faint orange. I gripped the Book of the Ancients tighter and glanced down at it, euphoric at the realization that we'd completed two parts of the spell, and that meant one thing: there was only one part remaining to finally annihilate Gérard's reign.

A sacrifice of will awaits
The last one standing behind the gates

12

OMEGA

"A sacrifice of will, what does that mean?" I shouted, turning to face Erica, Gabe and Audrey.

"Camille!" Dali's voice echoed over Gérard's roars from where he linked hands with Akim and Samira, eyes darting between me and the circle of fire in front of him. "Any day now would be lovely!"

I glanced down at the book again in frustration, waiting for the next illustration to light up and guide the way, but nothing appeared next to the golden arrow. Next to me, Erica screamed when frozen souls from the resistance and handfuls of guards began to take over the altar platform, moving up the throne stairs toward us, fighting one another as they did. Daggers were lodged into torsos, chests and necks, strikes and kicks thrown in every direction. Erica snatched Gabe and Audrey's hands and yanked them beneath the altar for cover. "Hurry, Camille, what does it say?" she yelled, covering her head.

"Nothing!" I shook it and grabbed my knives from

my belt, tossing the book to the floor. Combat couldn't wait. I caught a glimpse of Samira, Dali and Akim. Their eyes were shut, the light they'd been manipulating reappearing and growing brighter as they resumed their hold on Gérard. The circle's fire flared as their power grew, but I could tell by the struggle on their faces they wouldn't be able to hold him for much longer. The witches were lost in the shuffle in the center of the room, and as I scanned the floor for my friends, a guard slammed into me from the left, and then another, until I was taking them both on, my arms and daggers swinging from side to side in calculated swipes. One hand plunged a dagger into one's chest, and the other into another's thigh, my head ducking as one of the assailants retaliated, taking aim at my neck. I backed up and crashed into another enemy, and he spun around to take a stab at me, his strike even and focused. I dodged him and planted my boot into his midsection, then delivered a swift thrust into his heart with my dagger, just as Gavin had taught me. Smoke sizzled from his chest and the blade lodged deep, forcing me to yank and pull hard to release it.

Gavin's voice appeared from behind me, and then Arianna's.

"Camille, on your left!" he yelled.

"I got your right!" she hollered.

They saddled up to my sides and their knives smashed into the attackers while I confronted another who'd snuck up on me from behind. The three of us were now back-to-back, forming a small circle, knees bent and arms out, eyes darting everywhere. Frozen souls soared above us, pouncing and pummeling their enemies below, and Scarlet had swooped down in flight to attack Isa, first sinking her fangs into her neck and then shoving her blade tight into her side. Isa dropped to the ground in a pool of blood and Scarlet stared down at her in rage, nostrils flaring and stance like stone.

"The book!" Audrey shrieked from beneath the altar, pointing to the Book of the Ancients on the floor. She crawled out from beneath the table and scooped it up, squinting as its bright, golden light came to life. Josh appeared at the far side of the altar, charging a group of guards, but I didn't dare let my sight linger on him for long. I darted and crouched near the altar's edge to meet Audrey, Gavin and Arianna launching full force into another attack, their blades clacking and colliding with the enemy's blades while they continued to maneuver back-to-back.

"A sacrifice of will awaits, the last one standing behind the gates," Audrey read the words aloud to me as they danced across the last page. "Damn it, we know this already!" She threw her hands up in the air, shaking her head and flipping the pages. A shadow descended upon her, causing her head to snap upward and her eyes to bulge, her sight glued to something behind me.

"Cam …" she choked, raising her finger to point at the shadow. I swallowed and turned, raising my gaze, then gasping and rising to my feet.

A cloudy, near-transparent apparition stood before

me, the outline of its body fading in and out as it hovered off the ground. I'd recognize those discerning dark eyes anywhere.

"Vivienne," I mouthed, voice barely a whisper.

"It's called a sacrifice for a reason, nah, child," she said, her lips bunching, accentuating those familiar, faint wrinkles around her mouth. The sound of her voice was thin and distant, yet clear, each word that rolled from her lips annunciated and distinct. "It is the final retaliation of Gérard's magic against those who wish to defeat him, his last opportunity to exert control over his creations."

"I … I don't understand. What kind of sacrifice?"

The room's commotion quieted as her lips parted to respond, everyone's movements shifting into slow motion until they stilled completely. Vampires and humans were frozen in mid-battle, even Gérard, Samira, Dali and Akim coming to a halt, only the circle of fire flickering as it festered. The Book of the Ancients throbbed and emitted a low hum as its light continued to radiate from its pages, Audrey's stock-still hands gripping it tight.

"His magic secures the Amaranthian realm, and guarantees that it remain intact after he is destroyed … a tribute to his legacy, if you will."

My God, how highly this monster thought of himself.

"One must sacrifice their will, their freedom," she continued, "if they wish to destroy him. You'll have to decide who, nah, baby."

"Vivienne," I gulped, shifting forward to look at her ghost closely. "What are you saying?"

A ghoulish version of her arm stretched toward me and I flinched, not used to seeing spirits at all, let alone one move, speak, and reach out to touch me. "The sacrifice will break the curse and all will be set free, except for one—whoever makes the sacrifice and drives the dagger into Gérard's heart."

"Okay," I pushed a strand of loose hair behind my ear, "so whoever kills him remains a vampire? What if a human is the one to do it?"

Vivienne knowingly shook her head. "*Mmmm-mmm*. No, nah, baby. It doesn't work that way. Listen carefully, the ancestors sent me and my time is almost up, ya hear?"

I nodded, forced hard to swallow, knowing this was it—my last shot to get the answers I needed to save my friends.

"Whoever is in Amaranth when the curse is broken—and whoever strikes Gérard's heart—will remain caught in its realm for eternity."

All of the anxiety and anticipation harbored in the lines of my expression melted from my face, pulling my cheeks and the corners of my lips down into distraught weightlessness. My mind tried to register the implications of what she was saying, but all I could think was, *Who will do this?* "You mean …?"

"Yessum."

"Someone has to stay behind."

"The declaration of sacrifice must be made in the circle of fire. The moment his heart is pierced, the curse will be lifted, and all who remain with the one who slays him will never return to earth. The portal will be sealed off. No entry or exit."

Gravity.

That's all my body knew in that moment, already rooted to the floor, but now the ground was begging for more, enticing the full weight of my body to drop and meet the stone beneath it.

"But … that can't … it's not right. That can't be right." My fists curled tight at my sides and I started to shout. "No! It can't. That means … evil *wins*."

"Sometimes evil wins, nah, child. But it's always fleeting. Just a temporary ripple in a sea of goodness, brought on by the carnal nature of greed 'n corruption. Sacrifice washes that ripple out in waves of love 'n light, and peace is found when justice is served, even for those who lose, ya hear?"

"He shouldn't get a final say, shouldn't be able to retaliate like that! He was about to destroy this realm and create a brand new one! What does he care if this place continues to exist?"

"Of course not, baby, but nothin' you can do 'bout that, nah. Why do all bad things happen? None of them negate the good." She glided closer and peered down at me with so much love, I couldn't look away, desperate as I was to look anywhere but at the one whose eyes told me what I didn't want to hear. "Justice will still prevail," she said. "Don't forget what's given in place of that sacrifice, child. Make the call, baby." Her aura began to fade, her form flickering as it began to drift away.

"Vivienne, no … no, please wait!" The tears came and I dashed forward to follow her, but when I wiped them away, she was gone.

I spun around and crouched next to Audrey. She was still frozen and seated on the floor, the book clutched in her hands. I touched her shoulder and let another sob break free, hanging my head at the news I was about to deliver. Couldn't Vivienne have told Audrey, too? Couldn't she have let Gavin, Arianna, or Gabe hear what she had said? What about Erica, or even Dali and Akim, who I was sure would want to see Vivienne and hear it for themselves. They'd had ten times more invested in this curse, in this realm … in this mission, than I did. They'd been there since the beginning, watched as Gérard took over and held them captive with his magic in all sorts of ways.

A quiet rustling started to fill the room and I lifted my head. Everyone's movements slowly resumed around me. Rising to my feet, I ambled down the throne room steps. When I passed by them, I could feel Gavin and Arianna's movement as they finished off their attackers, but my sight was on the circle of fire before me and the magic that held Gérard inside it.

"Cam!" Gavin called out from behind me, but I kept moving.

Audrey joined him, screaming for me to hear her from the altar. I didn't look over my shoulder.

I scanned Dali, Akim and Samira's faces across the

flames as I came to stand behind Gérard, his back to me and arms outstretched as he fought to overpower their hold.

Dali's eyes shot to mine. "Well?" he yelled. "What did the bloody book say?"

I pressed my lips together and took a deep breath. "You all have to leave," I shouted. "Now!"

Akim hollered over the noise. "What?"

I raised my voice and turned in a circle, searching for my friends. "You all have to leave, do you hear me? Damn it, get out! Head for the portal now!" The riot was dying down all around us, many of the Amaranthians lost in the bloodshed, bodies of guards and frozen souls from the resistance on the ground, immobilized from dagger strikes. At one end of the altar, Josh struck a few more guards, while Gabe did what he could with his human strength to shoot daggers into some of the guards' chests. Audrey and Erica clutched one another beneath the altar, and I spotted Scarlet warring with a barrage of resistance vampires in the far corner of the room. I screamed louder, my entire frame shaking.

Gavin and Arianna rushed to my side and Gavin grabbed my face, eyes wide and jaw clenched tight. "Camille." When I didn't reply he gripped my cheeks tighter, imploring me to look at him. I tried pulling away from him, desperate for the others to see me, to hear me. "Talk to me, what did the book tell you?" he said. "Come on, baby, what's going on?"

I finally looked at him, the tears welling up and

pouring over my lids uncontrollably. "Whoever is here when the curse is lifted can never go back to earth: a sacrifice, the final requirement for the spell to work. Someone has to stay behind and take Gérard's life. Everyone else has to get out." I reached up and squeezed his forearms, and he immediately knew I was begging him to leave, because he grew so angry, the veins in his neck and forehead were bulging.

He gripped me back, shaking his head. "Don't even think about it!"

Arianna stepped closer, the haunted look on her face telling me she'd heard everything. "I'll do it."

Audrey, Gabe and Erica rushed over to join us, Josh swooping in behind them. "Do what?" Josh said.

Keeping one hand on the side of my head, Gavin twisted and grabbed Arianna's arm with the other, his eyes crazed. "Not happening, Ari. *Not happening,* do you hear me?" He turned back to me and the amount of affliction in his irises carved my insides with razor-blade sharpness. "This is my role. You have to go. Camille, look at me," he squeezed my shoulders, but I shook my head, adamant, moving to draw my blade.

Samira's voice bellowed in desperation, causing me to cry harder. "You fools! What on earth are you waiting for?"

I glanced around to see the remaining Amaranthians scurrying out of the throne room, likely heading toward the portal to escape while they could. Whether they'd heard my warning or sense was finally getting the better of them, I was thrilled they were leaving while they had the chance.

One more glance at Samira confirmed time was up. Her power had given out, and so had Dali's and Akim's. Gérard slumped on his knees in front of them, his eyes rolling upward as he attempted to crawl toward the edge of the flame. He groaned loudly when his fingertips reached the flames, weakness preventing him from going any farther.

Dali called out, slumping to the floor himself, hands shaking and shoulders sagging. "Amaranth is nearly drained, our energy depleted! Whatever you're going to do, do it now, will you?"

I pinned Gavin with my gaze and shot up on my tiptoes to sear him with a kiss, and it was a miracle I didn't collapse from the intensity of it and what it would mean to me for the rest of my life. It wasn't just a goodbye kiss. It was a there'll-never-be-another-like-you kiss, an I-want-the-best-for-you kiss that I prayed to God would sustain him when he went on to live a full, happy, human life back on earth. I knew it would be all of those things and so much more to me, but it was *his* heart I was yanking from his chest with my decision, and that's what mattered to me. I was giving up a piece of my own as well, but it was a choice.

His was just collateral.

Arianna stepped between us, grabbed my chin to force my gaze to hers. "I won't let you," she said.

"Let you what?" Audrey asked.

"Will someone please tell us what you're talking about?" Josh's voice was more frantic now.

"Gavin? Man?" Gabe piped up, Erica echoing him.

"Son? Look at me, son!" she then cried, latching onto Gavin's shoulder.

The throne room had emptied out, leaving just us, our little family, with so much to say and not enough time. Really, though, was there ever enough time?

The decision was simple, although the circumstance said otherwise: make the call.

I drew my dagger and gripped it firmly, breaking free from Gavin's grip and slipping through the circle of fire, Gérard at my feet.

"Cam!" Audrey flew forward to the edge of the flames, chest heaving under the weight of her panic. Gavin screamed and jumped inside the circle with me, pleading with tears covering his cheeks. I turned to face Audrey, and everything I loved was right there in her eyes, the memories tangible: the schooldays and sleepovers, the cheap bottles of wine and sappy chick flicks. She was there for my mother's drunken relapses, there to hold me until I fell asleep the first time the ex from Seattle hit me. It was all there, and my God, each memory was suddenly sacred and the sun rose and set upon it.

Those memories threatened to be my undoing, but I forced myself to focus. "Aud, I never told you what Cecile said to me right before—"

"No, Cam. No!"

"Listen to me. She said to make sure and tell you that

you were her angel."

"Why … why are you …?"

"I don't believe she said that just because she wanted you to know she loved you. You already knew she loved you. She said it because it was how she wanted to remember you—an angel, living on, even after she left this earth. That's what I want for you, Audrey. And it's what I need for me, do you understand?"

"No, no, no!"

Gabe and Josh's cries broke out now, the realization of what was happening shifting them into panic mode right alongside Audrey and Gavin.

Gabe called out to Gavin, "No man, no man—don't do this."

"I'll never forgive you if you stay," he replied. "Never. What was it all for, then, huh? Tell me."

"They want this." Arianna's voice silenced them, and she took their arms to back them away from the circle. "Don't deny them this. Joel would've wanted it, would've done the same thing." She released them and made her way around the circle to Samira, Dali and Akim. Samira's face was stricken with exhaustion, but the yearning was all over it: the desire to leave this place with her daughter. I shut my eyes in silent thanks when Arianna's voice lit up with the same hope, for the first time revealing a glimpse of forgiveness and compassion for her mother.

I jumped through the fire's edge and tackled Audrey in a hug as if she was the last breath of air on the planet. "I love you, Aud."

She quivered against me, her pleading words unintelligible at my ear, marred by the influx of sobs accompanying them.

"Now, go!" I released and shoved her, pushing her with ferocious effort, returning to the circle with Gavin. "Go, damn it! Go!"

Gavin exchanged looks with Samira and Arianna through the flames, then his mother, nodding and imploring them to leave. Arianna took hold of Samira and they turned for the doors, Gavin hollering at Josh and Gabe to follow. Gabe dragged Audrey away, stopping only to help lift Dali and Akim to their feet. Gabe forced Audrey to look away, his arm tight around her neck and shoulders as he guided her to the throne room doors, Dali and Akim sending us one last, grateful glance before limping along behind them. Erica placed a trembling hand to her lips and blew Gavin a kiss.

And then she was gone, leaving only echoes of Audrey's hysterical cries.

Gavin snatched my hand. "Are you sure you want to do this?"

"If you stay, it will all be in vain—"

"If I don't stay, it will all be in vain." He ran his thumb over the top of my wedding band, and then over my hip, over the exact location of the scar.

With a solid nod, I moved to hover over Gérard.

"Let me." Gavin stood next to me, pulling his knife from his belt.

"No, I volunteer for the sacrifice," I said, hoping such

a simple declaration would suffice. Sticking my boot into Gérard's side, I nudged and forced him to roll over so he was facing me. His tired eyes stared back at me, with no evidence of fear for the fact that his life was about to end. Instead, an arrogant grin teased his lips, the sight revolting.

"How does it feel?" he asked, droplets of sweat beading over his forehead and cheeks. "To know after all of this, you'll always be a slave to my world."

Every ounce of my desire for justice, and every empathetic strain of my heart, was charged into the look I gave him, thoughts of my friends, family, and countless innocents that had been affected by his greed, all swirling through my consciousness. How did it feel to be the one hanging over him with the weapon that would sentence him and free the ones I loved?

It felt *fantastic.*

I turned to look up at Gavin, a question in my eyes.

"I can't hear Josh anymore," he answered. "I think they're gone." Nodding, I stooped until my knees hit the floor. Gérard didn't deserve an answer to that question. But I gave him one anyway, for me, not for him. "I'll be a slave to love," I breathed, clasping the dagger tight between my fingers, raising it high above my head so I could peer down and see his final breath. "And you'll be … gone." With a steady, swift thrust, I shoved the dagger down and into his chest, until with a thick smack, it sank deep and lodged there.

Falling back, I caught myself with the heels of my

hands, watching in wonder as a shining golden light burst from the dagger's blade, casting an angelic, vertical beam that hit the throne room's ceiling. Gavin dropped behind me and scooped me into his lap, eyes trained on Gérard's body as it shriveled up and hardened before us. He tucked my head under his chin and rocked me slowly, fingers wiping the tears from my cheeks.

And then the tears were gone and his lips found mine. A tingling spark swept my body from head to toe.

"Do you feel that?" I jutted my head back to look at him.

"Yeah, I do...." His voice was hollow and everything turned to a blur. I blinked frantically, trying to fix my vision on his features, then on the room. Scanning my surroundings, the details became clearer, the tingling lessening and lifting from my body. Everything was light, from the inside out, all the heaviness dissipated.

"Cam?" Gavin pulled my head back to lock his gaze on mine, and when he did, I fell into his chest with tears and overwhelming bouts of laughter. He joined me and fell flat on his back, taking me with him. We laid there, our bodies shaking with delirium, and I took the opportunity to lazily bring my hand to his face, allowing my fingertips to graze his soft, human skin. My fingers skimmed his jawline and then over his chin, down to the curve of his neck, and I thought, *Yes, this is love*, and with a deep, satisfied breath, *the very thing that kept me mobile since the day I realized I was capable of giving and receiving it.*

EPILOGUE

Amaranth

The gray skyline outlined the emerald hills in the distance, and a soft wind stung my cheeks. Grasping the back of the wooden chair with a tired breath, I sat and gazed out at the windmill. The shuffling of footsteps on the cobblestone street stirred me from my midday, dreamy haze. Everything was so quiet and still, so peaceful, that even the slightest disturbance felt unnatural. Especially now, with the few of us that remained. Some of the Amaranthians hadn't made it out of the portal in time, and some were still hidden throughout the city's villages, having managed to evade the bloodshed that erupted due to the war. There were families hidden in the debris left behind in tattered pantries, cabinets, and just about every nook and cranny they could fit. Their ingenuity to hide and survive was more and more impressive each time we uncovered a new spot.

And then there were the remaining guards who

didn't make it out in time, who'd once answered to Samira and Gérard's every call. When their curses were lifted, they were trapped with us here, forced to help us rebuild a new village from the ground up, using what little supplies we had.

The shuffling footsteps grew closer and I twisted in my seat to turn and find their source. The movement left me winded.

"Hey, baby," Gavin said as he walked up the porch steps to plant a peck on my cheek. The flicker in his chocolate eyes brought a smile to my lips. I would never grow tired of seeing him human.

Never.

He bent down and kissed my belly. "And hey, baby." He smiled up at me, rubbing my stomach. He crouched down to kiss it again.

"Gav," I warned him, "don't start talking to it again, you already had a whole conversation with it this morning."

"It?" His brows shot up, his shy smile twisting his lips.

"It, my belly. You know what I mean." I ran my fingers through his hair, then leaned back in my chair, resigned to let him gab away if he'd keep glowing like that.

"It's okay, love. You're off the hook … for now. I have something I want to show you, come on." He stood and took my hand. "You won't have to walk far, I promise."

"Okay, where to?" I rose to my feet awkwardly, then waddled down the steps and let him lead the way.

"You'll see."

We moseyed down the main street hand in hand, ambling along as if we had all the time in the world. Well, we did have nothing but time. It was an odd feeling, one I still wasn't well acquainted with. The slow pace of our new lifestyle was jarring; transitioning from a non-stop race to save your life to a leisurely stroll in the park required quite the mental adjustment. Feeling Gavin's soft, human skin in my hand as we strolled along, I couldn't help but savor every second of our walk. I never wanted to take this gift for granted.

We stopped in front of one of the newly constructed shops. It was so modest and flimsy looking, I was afraid it might collapse when we walked inside. Looks were deceiving, though, because when we walked in, the surrounding walls and ceiling structure looked solid and cozy, and something smelled so good, my mouth watered.

"Is that ... oh my—"

"Chicken parmesan. Nice and fresh," Gavin answered, his face lighting up at my expression. "Come on back. I had to pay the guys down at the farm to bring me the poultry. They're thinking about opening a little butcher shop in the West Village. They have a good amount of livestock remaining, and the more magic they pick up, they might be able to increase their numbers."

He led me through the dim space to a cozy kitchen area in the back. Leaning to the window to open the shutters, he let hazy sunlight into the room, and I couldn't contain my surprise. "Gavin!"

"You like?" His timid grin appeared again, and he grabbed a towel from the stove handle to wipe his hands.

"Like it? Are you kidding? This is … this is *incredible*." He'd not only managed to arrange a shabby old stove in the corner, he'd built wood cabinets and countertops to create a fully functional kitchen. It was rustic and homey, and I didn't miss a single detail he'd included in the set-up. From the spice rack with our initials carved into the side to the hand-painted backsplash, I knew he'd put his heart and soul into this kitchen. I scanned the stovetop again, inhaling deeply the scent of his signature pasta sauce, but froze when I spotted the framed photo above the stove.

"What do you think?" he said. "I thought … you know."

My words caught in my throat as I studied the picture in the clunky straw frame. It was an old shot of Audrey and Gabe back in Louisiana, Gabe's arms casually wrapped around Aud's shoulders, her head thrown back in uninhibited laughter. Gabe's eyes were on her, and I think it was Gavin who had taken the shot, because a sauce-covered wood spoon was obstructing the side of the lens, its blurry silhouette cutting off the left side of Audrey's head. "One of the nights you were cooking for them back at your place?" I said.

"Yeah, I finally managed to snatch the pot from Audrey and take over the kitchen again. She was throwing a fit over the sauce that night and wouldn't let me cook. She was driving me crazy, and Gabe was useless." He laughed fondly. "He was just sitting around, getting a kick out of our bickering."

"Sounds like Gabe. And Audrey was certainly Queen of Throwing Fits." I joined him in soft laughter and stepped closer to the frame, reaching out to stroke it, as if it were a medium to all the life in that photograph. "I love it, Gav. I'm blown away that you did all this. Isn't it the mom who's supposed to be nesting or whatever? And here you are, building us a kitchen."

"Nah," he took my hand, "there's more to it than that. Follow me."

"More?"

"*Mmmhhhmm*."

He led me back out the way we came, moving to the main windows to push open the heavy shutters. Light poured in and danced across four round pub-like tables in the center of the room. Shaggy tan linens covered them, and each one had a single red rose in the center, each propped up in an old tin can. Gavin strolled to the far end of the room and stepped up onto a chair to reach a sheet-like covering that hung from the top of the wall, over a counter that opened up to the kitchen area we'd just come from. Yanking it down, he shook out the dust and gave his very best "ta-da" presentation, turning to catch my expression.

Although the sunlight was minimal in the room, I could make out each bright red letter painted on the wall: "Audrey's Kitchen." To the left, behind the chair Gavin stood on, was a tiny, triangle-shaped stage tucked into the room's corner, an acoustic guitar propped up against the wall. Noticing my appraisal of the stage, Gavin stepped down from the chair and picked up the guitar, wiping the dust off.

"Arianna and Joel would want music here," he said. "I can cook, and people can come in and play while I serve the food. I made a menu based off Gabe's favorites. He was Audrey's biggest fan, so ..."

"Gavin ..." My hand cupped my mouth and I braced myself on the back of one of the chairs. "They would love this."

"I think so, too." He smiled, crossing the room to wrap me in his arms. Our embrace was interrupted when two women appeared at the door, knocking softly on the frame to announce their presence.

"Greta?" Gavin pulled back and turned to them. "Denise? What's up?"

"There's something happening in the castle you should see," Greta spoke up, wiping her hands on her apron. "Well, you both should see, although I'm not sure Camille is up for a trek up that hill."

"No, I don't think she is," he answered, wiping his stubbly jaw. "I'll come on up though, is everything okay?"

"I think so...." Greta exchanged a nervous glance with Denise, and I perked up.

"It's not anything to do with *him*, is it?" I said. We'd buried the remains of Gérard's ashes behind the castle, first giving the fallen members of the resistance their own graves and burials to pay our respects. Still, simply having remnants of him close by gave me chills.

"Oh heavens no," Greta said, "nothing like that."

Gavin peered down at me and we all took a collective sigh of relief. "Good," he said, walking to the door to follow them out.

"Wait. I want to go with you."

Greta's eyebrows shot up and she looked to Gavin. "Honey, you're about to pop," she said. "Are you sure?"

"Yeah, Gavin will help me." I squeezed his hand. "I might move a little slow, but I want to see what all the fuss is about."

Denise and Greta couldn't hold back their girlish glee. It was too cute to deprive them of it, and I really did want to know what was going on up at the castle. Gavin and I hadn't visited since the burials.

After a tiring walk up the valley's hill, we passed through the dirt-trodden path where the gates once stood and made our way inside the castle, to the main throne room. Samira's altar had been repurposed, covered in potions, herbs, and all sorts of materials taken from Dali and Akim's windmill bunker. Their spell books and supplies had been moved here, and now the space was used as a sort of workshop and library, where the remaining humans could learn about the witches' history and learn how to conjure. So far, we'd learned how to use the magic for food and other necessities. The results weren't always perfect; sometimes we'd wind up with a bucket of fish when we were shooting for some eggs, but we were making progress, and beggars couldn't be choosers.

Behind the altar, on each side of the fireplace sat two massive bookshelves the men had built to store all the resources from the haven. Some of the shelves housed more books, ones that taught us about the ancients and their magic, while others shelved historical artifacts and the remaining supplies that had been horded in the haven for emergencies. Our dream was to create a mecca of information for the humans living here, knowledge that would someday be passed on to their children and their children's children. I for one never wanted my child to wonder about her parents' history, or the history of the frozen souls or witches.

Admiring the throne room's transformation when we entered brought me great satisfaction, and the pride on Gavin's face told me he felt the same.

"So what're we looking for?" he asked Greta and Denise.

"Come with us," Denise said, waving.

We followed them out the main doors and toward the moat, out onto the main castle lawn. We were greeted by a crowd of people in front of an amazing sight: a tall, elegant sculpture of Gavin and me. The figures were locked in an embrace. My long hair blew dramatically to the side, and Gavin's forehead was pressed tenderly to mine. Denise moved forward, pulling a sheet from the foot of the sculpture to reveal a wooden plaque, the title "The Devereauxs" carved whimsically across the front.

Greta, Denise, and the others moved in closer,

holding out their hands to present us with an array of gifts for the baby and for our new home. We were overwhelmed with baskets of cheese and luscious grapes, knitted pink-colored booties and bonnets, and all kinds of sweet-smelling candles. The emotion overtook me, and whether it was my hormones or the essence of their gestures, it didn't matter. The dam broke and the tears flowed, and I reached out to accept what I could. Gavin did the same, laughing and thanking people quicker than the words could catch up with his acknowledgements.

"This is your kingdom, now," Greta announced, the dimples around her smile twinkling. "We owe our freedom and our loyalty to you."

Humility washed over Gavin's face. "No. You don't."

I spoke up, my words strained. "None of you made it out of here."

A chorus of disagreement erupted from the crowd.

"We made it out of here," Greta tapped her forehead, "and now we reside here," she added, clutching her chest.

"Yes," Denise chimed in, her gaze bouncing between Gavin and me. "You of all people can relate to the peace of the heart: what it means to be set free from the burdens of the mind. You've lost your friends and families as well, but you've found peace, yes?"

I squeezed Gavin's hand. "Yes."

"So then accept our tribute and our loyalty." She beamed, gesturing to the gifts surrounding us. "It's your kingdom now!"

A burly man stepped forth, his beard bristling against

his lips as he spoke. "We declare a new era and a new king and queen."

"Here, here!" another shouted.

At the men's words, everyone bent to drop down on one knee and bow. The sky above the sculpture erupted in a loud crack as the clouds started to scatter, revealing a seraphic under layer of baby blue. Everyone's heads snapped up in awe as the grayish haze, which had been a constant throughout the realm, atomized and unleashed waves of warm sunlight over the castle's grounds. Our gazes followed the clouds as they continued to disintegrate in a rolling motion, past the castle's horizon, over the hills, and out over the valley, lighting up the emerald lands until the entire city was drowned in voluptuous light. We'd bid our days on earth goodbye and lost much in the tragedies of the journey, but the beauty that lay before us now was far from those bittersweet farewells.

It was the future. Ever forward. *Always ever forward.*

Fear is Sabotage's Sweetest Weapon

PRESERVATION

RACHAEL WADE

AVAILABLE NOW AT AMAZON.COM

PRESERVATION

Available in print and e-book from Amazon.com and in print from BarnesAndNoble.com.

An Adult Contemporary Romance

Fear is sabotage's sweetest weapon.

Kate has no time for meaningless romantic charades, and definitely no time for hot college professors who are full of themselves and smitten with her. Constantly battling eviction notices, tuition she can't afford, and a sick, dependent mother, the last thing she needs is to be distracted with someone else's complicated baggage.

When she stumbles into Ryan Campbell's creative writing class, he is only "Mr. Campbell" to her, until Ryan finds himself captivated by her writing and she is forced to face their mutual attraction. His cocky know-it-all syndrome is enough to send her running in the other direction, and his posse of female admirers and playboy reputation are enough to squander any odds in her favor.

But underneath Ryan's abrasive facade is something to behold, and she can't stay away for long. Ryan and Kate must decide who they're willing to become and fight against their former selves if they want to make things work. That's if academia, vicious vixens, old skeletons, and their own mastery at self-destruction don't pummel their efforts first.

978-0-9840208-4-3 ~ www.RachaelWade.com

REPOSSESSION

Book One of *The Keepers Trilogy*

A New Post-Apocalyptic Sci-Fi Romance Series

Skylla only knows that she has been kidnapped and held hostage by the foreign invaders and their human allies. And that the world is ending. Or so the humans think. The invaders have made it clear that their arrival is one of hostile intent, and as their takeover spreads, so does the panic across the globe. No one knows how to defeat them, or if it's even sane to try.

Jet, Skylla's human captor, is up for the challenge, though. A traitor in Skylla's eyes, he is working with them. But Jet has his own agenda; one that doesn't include babysitting Skylla or helping the enemies. And as the human race struggles to keep the invaders from achieving their goal, Jet and Skylla's paths collide to reveal the truth behind Skylla's abduction.

The invaders are headed for the water. Jet is headed for the water. But that's the last place Skylla wants to be. That's where the future of humanity lies, and where the bridge to their yesterdays was burned. On a mission to take back what is rightfully theirs, Earth's population is determined to make sure this isn't the end. But some endings were never theirs to begin with.

REPOSSESSION

RACHAEL WADE

COMING 2013

CPSIA information can be obtained at www.ICGtesting.com
Printed in the USA
LVOW060728171012

303177LV00001B/53/P